A WOLF'S PROMISE

A GAY SHIFTER ROMANCE

NOAH HARRIS

A WOLF'S PROMISE

A Gay Shifter Romance
Family Secrets Book Six

Noah Harris

Published by BUP LLC, 2018.

This book is a work of fiction. All resemblance to persons living or dead is purely coincidental.

This book contains sexually explicit scenes and adult language and may be considered offensive to some readers. Please don't read if you are under eighteen.

CHAPTER 1

"Looks like a jungle out there."

Dean's gaze lingered on the tangled chaos in front of him. The season had been kind, and the grass and weeds had grown tall and wild. It was hard to tell where the grass ended and the weeds began. They were so twisted around one another it was almost impossible to tell.

"Kinda have to agree with you," Dean said.

Silun turned away from the overgrown mess. "And you want us to clear it out?"

"That's the idea."

It had seemed like a good idea when he'd first suggested it. He owned plenty of land that was still uncultivated. He would never end up using it all, as there was far too much. He was only one man and as helpful as Mikael was, the man was busy at this time of year. It was meant to be a simple clearing job, mowing down the wilderness to find some relatively flat land to build on. Now, it was looking a little trickier than he'd originally thought.

"You sure your Druid powers don't make everything grow really well?" Silun asked.

Dean shrugged. "I doubt whatever weird effect people say I have is just limited to the useful plants."

"Dude, you can talk to plants. You told me that yourself, so it's not just everyone else saying it."

Dean smiled at the casual protest in Silun's voice. The teenager had been coming around the farm a lot more lately. He'd been too weak and unsettled to leave the Grove after his rescue from the clutches of Damian in the bowels of the mountain. By the time summer arrived, Silun started showing up around the farm more often. Whatever horrors he experienced at the hands of Damian and his goons hadn't seemed to put Silun off his stride.

Dean respected that sort of resiliency.

"Yes, but I meant where people think everything grows better automatically just by being around me. But after seeing the harvest last fall, and now looking at this, I'm beginning to wonder," Dean explained with a sigh. If there was a way to make it work only on the plants he wanted to grow, he needed to find it. Silun was only voicing what Dean had already thought. Now he was wondering if all the extra weeding he had to do this year really was due to his druid influence.

"You could always talk to the weeds, couldn't you?" Silun asked, eyeing the foliage.

"And say what? 'Please don't grow here.' I'm not sure how that would work. Plus, I would probably have to talk to each and every damn weed while I'm at it. Easier to just get rid of them when they appear and move on."

"Wait, now I have to ask. Do you like, hear the plants when you're weeding them?"

Dean winced at the thought. "Thankfully no. Just like you can turn off hearing spirits when they decide to get chatty, I can turn off hearing plants. It would be a nightmare otherwise. How's that coming along by the way?"

Silun looked at Dean once more, and Dean realized the shaman was already as tall as him. It was enough to make him sigh all over again. Being a few inches shy of average height, Dean had grown used to other guys being taller than him. At least the law of averages was on his side, and he would run into men his height or shorter. When it came to werewolves however, tall seemed to be etched into their genetic structure. Even a lot of the women were taller than him.

"What, listening to the spirits?" Silun asked.

Dean nodded. "You haven't seen any other shamans, and you haven't really talked about what happened."

It was Silun's turn to shrug. "It's alright. My master was a good teacher. He taught me enough that I can get by. That book you gave me has helped a lot though, so thank you for that. I've been taking really good care of it."

"I appreciate that. I pretty much have it memorized anyway. It's better if a shaman has hold of it and I think Talon would be happy with you having it. He, uh, hasn't by any chance, done one of those ancestor visit things, has he?"

Silun shook his head. "No. I'm sorry, Dean. It's really rare for the spirit of a werewolf to visit another, even a shaman. I'm pretty sure he's gone to the Summerlands by now."

"Summerlands?"

"You've been doing all this reading on werewolf lore and shamans and you haven't come across the Summerlands? I guess I should have looked into what Samuel and Matalina are teaching over in the Grove, huh?"

Dean grinned at that. "I would love to see you try and tell Samuel what he should and shouldn't be teaching. I'm sure that would go over really well. And no, is that like, werewolf Heaven or something?"

"Basically. It's a land of plenty, rife with prey, where the forest is never ending, and a werewolf can live free."

"Sounds nice, but it really doesn't sound like something Samuel would be big on teaching. The guy might be a werewolf, and know that all sorts of supernatural stuff exists, but he doesn't strike me as the spiritual type. But, is there by any chance a werewolf Hell, too?" Dean asked, his mind flashing to Damian.

"Not really. Any werewolf who is found unworthy to walk the Summerlands, you know, betrayers, kin-slayers, murderers, etc. don't get to go there. Instead they apparently have to wander the places between worlds, lost and alone forever."

"Sounds close enough to me," and, he thought, no less than someone like Damian deserved. The former alpha had done nothing but cause chaos and pain in the little time Dean had known him. Then he used kidnapped shamans to fuel a crystal to gain power to serve his own ambitions. It had been cut short when Dean interfered, ending with him stabbing Damian and sending him falling into a pit in the collapsing depths of the mountain. Dean told himself Damian deserved nothing less, and that the world was better for his absence.

It didn't do anything for the twist in his gut when he thought about it, however. Any more than thinking about the death of Scar, the jailer Damian had been using in the mountain, did. Dean knew his only choice had been to fight his way out, or end up a plaything for Damian's pleasure. The jailer hadn't exactly been a good person either, just one more sadist in Damian's pack. Yet the memory of the blood splattered cage Dean had been held in haunted him still.

Scar's death might have been necessary, but it had also been messy.

"Dean?"

Dean's head jerked up. "What?"

"I asked if you wanted to get started. Are you okay?"

"Yeah, sorry. Just got lost in my thoughts I guess. There's still a lot to do; trying to wrap my head around it."

Silun frowned at him, with a disbelieving look. "You sure? You got this really...scary look on your face?"

That surprised Dean. "Scary?"

"Yeah, you thinking about the mountain?"

Dean shook his head, perhaps more vehemently than he needed to. "No."

"You know you can talk to me about that stuff, right? I know I'm just a kid to you, but I'm here for you too. It's the least I can do. I owe you for saving my ass like you did."

"You also saved Apollo's life, so I think that makes us even."

"You dragged me out of a prison cell in a mountain where I probably would have spent the rest of my life if you hadn't come along?"

Dean had no intention of talking about what happened in that mountain. Not with Silun, and not with anyone else for that matter. The threat of Damian and what he'd been attempting was over and he wanted to move past it. The past year had been filled with enough horrors to fuel his nightmares for the next decade, at the very least. Now he wanted to get something good out of all of it, and fully appreciate the things he had earned.

"I'm okay Silun, I swear."

"Uh huh, I might be young but I'm not dumb. And I know I'm not the only one who's noticed. You're not talking to Mikael about it either, are you?"

Dean's jaw tightened. "There's nothing to talk about. And what I do or do not talk about with my mate is none of your concern, Silun."

The young werewolf held his hands up in a gesture of surrender. "Alright, okay. I'll leave you alone about it. Just, please, talk about it eventually, okay? Nobody can go through all that and not need to get it off their chest eventually."

Dean squinted up at him. "Uh huh, and who have you been talking to?"

At that, Silun blushed. "Dante."

"Really? Wow, I would have expected Apollo, or maybe even Matalina. Dante? Really? The same werewolf who gets grumpy and swears a lot?"

Silun frowned. "He's not that bad, he can be really nice. You just got off on the wrong foot with the whole 'fight over Mikael' thing."

"Heard about that, huh?"

Silun nodded. "Do you not like him?"

"I like him just fine, but he didn't strike me as the type to let someone cry on their shoulder is all. He's a good guy. He just has a temper."

Silun's blush didn't disappear. "I didn't *cry*. We just, you know, talked."

The bashful tone of Silun's voice piqued Dean's interest. "Wait, do you have a crush on the guy?"

At that, Silun turned completely red in the face. "Dean!"

Dean laughed. "You do! Lord, wasn't Katarina enough?"

At the reminder of his short-lived crush on Katarina, Silun turned away from Dean. He knew it was so Silun could hide whatever mortified expression he had on his face. He'd admitted to Dean about his crush on Katarina after being in the Grove for a couple of weeks. Those hadn't been the teenager's exact words, but a crush is what it was nevertheless. Dean didn't know why it had petered out, but it had, and before the summer was in full swing. Now, it seemed like Silun's feelings were swinging toward a different, if equally brusque werewolf.

"It's not like that!" Silun protested, his back still to Dean.

"Hey. I'm sorry I laughed," Dean apologized, meaning it. "I just wasn't expecting you to get a crush on Dante is all. He's not what I would consider the soft and cuddly type."

"I just like him a little. Just a little. I know it's not a big deal or anything. He's way older than me, I'm still a kid to you guys. It's just, well, a crush, like you said. A teenage crush."

Dean curled an arm around one of Silun's elbows. "Hey, don't put yourself down like that. You're more mature at your age now than I bet most of the pack were at the same age."

"I notice you didn't disagree with anything else I said."

Dean winced. "Look, it's obvious, now anyway, that you swing both ways. That's upping your chances of finding someone perfect for you, right?"

"I don't think it works like that, Dean."

"No, probably not. But do you really want me to give you platitudes about how you'll find the right guy or girl? Or that this too will pass? Darkest before the dawn?"

Silun laughed, "Please don't."

"See?"

Silun gave their entwined arms a warm squeeze. "It's alright. Even if I was older or something, he's not going to pay attention to me. I'm pretty sure he's already got his eyes set on someone else."

"Again with the surprises. He didn't strike me as the crush having type either. Do tell."

Silun shook his head. "No way. I don't even know if I'm right, because it's hard to tell. But if I am right, I'm not going to go around telling everyone his business like that."

Dean turned them away from the overgrown patch of land. "Oh, you're no fun at all. A little bit of gossiping is bound to make you feel better."

Silun opened his mouth to protest further and then stopped, squinting in the direction of the farmhouse. "Who's that, at your house?"

Dean stood taller, looking into the distance. "Oh boy, that's the Williams' truck. You're in for a treat."

"Uh, the Williams'?"

"Neighbors. And Mrs. Williams is going to *love* you."

CHAPTER 2

The conversation from the living room was floating nicely into the kitchen as he worked marinating a few steaks. The Williams' had, in fact, been delighted with Silun after being introduced. They hadn't had the chance to meet him before, despite his numerous visits. They weren't supposed to be staying for long, and the large amount of meat he was prepping was mainly for Silun and Mikael. Werewolf fast metabolism meant they ate enough to feed a teenage boy or two, doubly so in Silun's case.

His mind drifted to Mikael, making him smile. It was their first summer of being truly together, and he was missing Mikael's almost constant presence. The summer season was a busy one, and Dean's mate hadn't been around as much as usual. Both of them had to adjust to not seeing one another so often, but they usually made up for it when Mikael came home.

Dean was happy for him, though. He knew Mikael loved his work and would miss it when he had to spend more time in the Grove after he eventually became Alpha. It didn't hurt that Dean had seen him work more than once.

The contentment on Mikael's face as he carefully built or repaired something filled Dean with joy, a feeling he kept to himself. The sight of Mikael's muscles working, skin covered in a light sheen of sweat from the summer sun, was an altogether different sort of joy.

"I think she's ready to adopt him," Mr. Williams told him as he entered the kitchen.

Dean flipped on the water to wash his hands. "She does know he has a family, right? That he's only staying with Mikael's family for a little while?"

Mr. Williams helped himself to the warm coffee pot. "Doesn't change that she's got that look in her eye. Says she's ready to carry him outta here herself."

Dean laughed as he dried his hands. "I told him you two would like him. He's a good kid."

"He's a dear," Mrs. Williams proclaimed as she walked in behind her husband. She frowned at the coffee cup in his hand, but said nothing. Dean remembered that Mr. Williams blood pressure wasn't the best, which explained why the older man was raiding his coffee supply. Mrs. Williams had promptly switched them over to decaf; something Dean told Mikael was forbidden in their home. Better dead than decaf.

Sensing the possible storm, Mr. Williams retreated from the room. Dean watched him go with a smirk. He knew he probably shouldn't enable the man, but he wasn't going to get involved either. If Mr. Williams wanted to pillage their supply of coffee when he was here, Dean wasn't going to stop him.

"How long will he be staying?" Mrs. Williams asked as she dug out the jug of tropical fruit juice. Dean guessed the older woman was getting Silun something to drink. His prediction about Silun bringing out her maternal side was proving to be true.

"I didn't ask," Dean lied smoothly as he busied himself with cleaning up. Truth was, they hadn't heard anything back from the pack Silun had belonged to. It was possible they had moved due to the war, or worse, had been wiped out. All the packs were still in a state of chaos as they tried to settle everything Damian had stirred up. It wasn't all out war anymore, but some packs were still seizing the opportunity to attack rivals who they thought might be ripe for the picking. As a result, news was scattered and they just hadn't heard anything back yet. So, for however long it took to get some answers, Silun was an honored guest of the Grove.

"And he's staying with you and Mikael?"

"He stays here every once in a while. He likes it out here, and we don't mind having him around."

"Don't you think he's a little young to be staying with you two?"

The thin tone of disapproval in her voice brought Dean up short. He turned to see the emotion on her face as she eyed him carefully. Confusion was all he felt for a moment, trying to figure out what he had done wrong. His mind replayed what she had said only a moment before, and his eyes widened in horror.

"Mrs. Williams! He's sixteen!"

"Is he?" She asked, looking surprised. "I thought he was a few years older than that. I swear, as I get older, I can't tell the difference. He could have been your age for all I know."

Dean gaped. "Yeah, he's sixteen. I thought you knew that because your husband made a joke about you adopting him."

Mrs. Williams waved the jug of juice at him dismissively. "You can legally adopt an adult Dean. Or at least I heard you can. I suppose it would just be a change of your last name, but still."

Dean shook his head, freezing as another idea came to him. "Wait. Is that what you thought was happening when Apollo was here?"

"Well, I didn't want to ask. You did introduce him as Mikael's cousin, but around here, everyone is everyone's cousin. They're not actually related, but..."

Which was true in this case too but, "Mrs. Williams! Mikael and I are completely monogamous, we would never..."

She held up her hands. "As you say, Dean. I didn't mean to upset you. I wasn't about to pass judgement on whatever you two do in your private moments. I apologize about Silun. I thought he was older, since he certainly acts nothing like any teenager I ever knew."

Dean groaned, now seriously contemplating the beer in the fridge. "Mrs. Williams, please."

"It was an honest mistake."

Dean's face was now flushed with embarrassment, thinking it was anything but an honest mistake. He had no idea what he or Mikael had done to give her the idea that they were anything but monogamous. After this conversation, he wasn't sure he really wanted to hear the reasoning behind her opinion either. Mrs. Williams certainly looked like an innocent, grandmotherly type, but the woman was brutally honest and about as subtle as a sledgehammer. If he asked, he was going to get an answer, and he wasn't sure he wanted one.

"Good heavens, is this for all of you?" She asked, as she replaced the juice, pointing at the bag of marinating steaks.

"There's two full grown, hardworking men in this

house, and a teenage boy who's been roped into helping me. We have big appetites."

"You're certainly doing well if you can afford meals like that," she commented as she closed the fridge door. "Which is good. I'm happy to see you're doing well. For the most part."

Dean raised a brow. "For the most part?"

"Sweetheart, please tell me you aren't about to start on at him about marriage," Mr. Williams chided her, reappearing in the doorway, this time with Silun in tow.

Dean stared at her. "Please tell me you aren't going to have a conversation about marriage with me, Mrs. Williams. Because that's really too close to Mikael making an honest man out of me, for my liking."

She huffed. "Well I am sorry if I just want to see you two hitched. You've been living together long enough, haven't you? I know, you haven't even been together for a year yet, but that didn't stop him from moving in with you, now did it? Or from you spending all that time with his family. I'd say it's about time."

"Mrs. Williams," Dean protested, sounding pained. "It will happen when it happens."

"I just want to see you happy, Dean."

Dean motioned around him, his hands spread wide. "Happy? I've got a beautiful house, fertile land, I'm comfortable financially, I have more family than I know what to do with, and a man who is devoted and madly in love with me. How can I not be happy?"

"You just look...tired to me."

The last was said quietly, the force of her voice gone and replaced only by unfiltered concern. Caught off guard, Dean glanced between Mr. and Mrs. Williams. Silun hung behind Mr. Williams, the older man looking uncomfortable.

His lack of comment told Dean he didn't disagree with his wife's assessment. She wasn't even looking at her husband. She was looking at her feet, and that worried Dean more than anything.

Out of the corner of his eye, he saw Silun slip out of the room. Dean couldn't blame him, the mood in the room had taken a swift downturn. Dean was more surprised she had even brought it up in the first place with Silun around. Before this, he would have bet money that she would have waited until they were alone to bring it up.

"I haven't been sleeping much and there's a lot to do, Mrs. Williams. I'm trying to get this farm up to scratch, up to where I need it to be."

She shook her head. "It's more than that, Dean. You just seem...a little different."

Now he was really worried; she sounded downright upset. "Mrs. Williams, I'm fine."

She looked up at him for a moment, then looked to Mr. Williams. He looked just as lost as she did, shrugging his broad shoulders. First Silun had been concerned, and now he had his well-meaning neighbors worrying over him. The only person who had been around him who hadn't said anything, was Mikael. Was his mate just keeping his mouth shut, trying to allow Dean the illusion of privacy? If the people who only *saw* him were worried, what was going on in the head of the man who could sometimes *feel* what Dean was feeling?

"You were lookin' tired when you got back before winter," Mr. Williams explained. "But we figured it was because you were banged up. But it ain't gone away, just got worse. We're worried, Dean."

Dean gestured helplessly. "It's been a busy year. There's been a lot going on. Maybe I could be sleeping more, but it's nothing like...please tell me this isn't you guys thinking Mikael is the cause."

Mr. Williams shook his head. "No. Honestly, I think that man is the only reason you're still goin' sometimes. You just look like a man who's at the end of his rope. You got that thousand-yard stare I seen sometimes, after the war."

Now there was a term Dean hadn't actually heard used outside of books. It was probably the same look Silun had been talking about out in the field. Now he had the Williams' looking at him like he was one step away from losing his mind.

So what if he had been having nightmares that kept him from sleeping? They would pass, in time. Sometimes, he got lost thinking about the look on Damian's face when he saw the blade heading for his hand, sending him to his death. Other times, it was all the blood in the cell, or the acceptance of death on Talon's face. Day and night, these thoughts came to him, but they passed and would eventually stop haunting him.

They had to.

The sound of the front door opening interrupted any response he might have had. Mikael's familiar rumble echoed down the hallway. The sound of his mate's voice instantly removed the tension from the room. Dean smiled at the two of them as he heard Mikael speaking quietly with Silun in the hallway.

"And just like that," Mrs. Williams breathed, eyeing Dean critically.

"What?" Dean asked.

"I told you," Mr. Williams said pointedly to his wife.

Mrs. Williams only shook her head. "I know you did; no need to rub it in."

Dean stared in confusion between them. "Did I miss something?"

"Just that you looked like you were about ready to drop on the spot. Then he comes home and suddenly you look even better than when you first came here," Mrs. Williams explained, plucking the glass of juice up from the counter.

"Well, that's love, isn't it?" Dean asked.

"That it is. I hope it's enough," and without another glance, she left the kitchen to continue doting on Silun.

"This," Dean began, looking at Mr. Williams, "isn't over, is it?"

Mr. Williams huffed. "Naw, not with my wife it isn't. I kept her quiet all winter, and even during the spring. But you ain't gonna be able to avoid her for long if she can help it."

"Mr. Williams..."

The older man held up a hand. "I know. You're entitled to keep your business to yourself. But we consider you family Dean, and family gets nosey sometimes. She ain't gonna let you get away with this if you don't get back to looking like yourself again."

"Mr. Williams, I'm fine. I just need to work on sleeping some more or something."

"Or something," Mr. Williams replied, glancing over his shoulder at the sound of slow footsteps.

Mikael entered, glancing between Dean and Mr. Williams. There was no expression on his face, but Dean could see the wheels of his mind turning. Mikael looked at Dean sensing something was going on, and trying to figure out what he'd missed. Dean only gave him a little shrug in return. He had already gone through two of those conversations today, he didn't want to go for round three this early.

Telling Mikael could come later, when there wasn't an audience.

"You're home early," Dean told Mikael, loving the way he stalked towards him.

"Finished the porch early," Mikael told him, standing before Dean. His eyes were searching Dean's face, and Dean was pretty sure he was searching his inner voice as well. That emotional bond between them from their mating provided a few nifty tricks, one of which was the ability to sense the emotional welfare of the other. Mikael had taken to searching those depths with remarkable ease, where Dean still struggled to consciously do so. Dean thought it had to do with Mikael being a werewolf, while Mikael just said Dean had trouble letting go of control.

"Why are you glaring at me like I did something wrong?" Mikael asked, sounding amused.

Dean straightened out his face, not realizing his thoughts were so obviously showing. "Just thinking about how much of a brat you can be sometimes."

"I had better go save that boy before she talks his ear off," Mr. Williams quipped, and Dean listened as his heavy footsteps disappeared down the hallway.

"I miss something?"

Mikael's question had Dean shaking his head. "Mrs. Williams being her usual self. I'll tell you later, when there aren't quite as many ears around."

"Alright."

His hello kiss was soft, though a little hesitant. Dean read the wariness Mikael must have been feeling in that kiss. This was bound to go one of two ways. Either Mikael would approach the subject later, if he felt it was safe to do so, or he would leave it alone if he thought Dean needed space. Dean appreciated that Mikael took each of these moments on a case-by-case basis. The downside being that he never knew which case would result in what decision.

"We should probably go help Mr. Williams save Silun," Dean leaned around Mikael to listen for any warning signs.

"She's already threatened to take him clothes shopping," Mikael informed him, sounding like he was about to laugh.

"Lord, let's save him before it's too late."

CHAPTER 3

B lood. It was always blood. The smell of it was thick and cloying, from his nose to the back of his throat. The coppery taste filled his mouth, making him gag. There was too little light to make out exactly what he and the ground were coated with. To him, it didn't matter if the warm slickness appeared black or not, he could taste what it was.

A sickening blue light pulsed somewhere around him, making the blood look blacker. He knew that light and he knew this room. It was bigger than he remembered, the ceiling and walls extending beyond even the reach of the pulsing blue light. Somewhere out there, people, things, were moaning. They said his name, cried out words he couldn't make out, screaming for vengeance.

He was alone here; he knew that. Everyone was gone, either dead or they had left him behind. All there was for him was being stuck in this hell of alternating darkness and horrible blue light. He shivered against the cold air that filled the cavern, the chill sinking past his skin and into his bones. The only warmth was the constant trickle of tears that ran down his face. Even his tears couldn't save him here. This was where he would find an end to the beginning he had started. Bathed in blood, and lost in the dark, he would finally reap what he had sown.

"Dean!"

A voice cried out from the darkness, echoing up into the reaches of the unseen roof. Something grabbed him from behind, the grip iron tight on his shoulder. The cry of fear was ripped from him as the unseen hands tried to pull him backwards. He fought against it, knowing that as bad as it was, going into the darkness would be even worse. Another hand wrapped around his chest, pulling him back further into the darkness.

"Dean! It's me!"

His eyes snapped open and he squinted against the moonlight that came streaming through a familiar window. This was his room, not the seemingly infinite depths of a mountain. The press of the bed against him was far warmer than the hard cold of the cave floor he had been dreaming of. It was a dream. Of course it was a dream. That cavern was gone, buried beneath the mountain. He was never going to have to physically go anywhere like that again, if only the same could be said for his mind.

The phantom that had grabbed him in his dream was Mikael. The werewolf was holding on to him, keeping his body pressed tight to Dean. Their breathing was ragged, Mikael's breaths were harsh gusts of warm air against his neck. His nightmare had leaked into the waking world, enough to have woken Mikael from his own dreams.

"Dean?"

His throat was dry, but he managed to whisper a quick, "Yeah, I'm okay."

Mikael didn't let go of him, however. He merely shifted his grip around Dean's body. No longer trying to hold Dean back from whatever he might have been doing, Mikael wrapped his arms around him in a comforting grip. One strong arm curled under his shoulder to hold him tight while the other one curled about his waist. Neither was enough to hide the fact that he was still shaking. They didn't disguise the sweat coating his body and the smell of fear, either.

"I'm sorry," he finally managed, trying to wet his throat by swallowing.

"Hey," Mikael murmured, his thumb rubbing a circle on Dean's waist. "Don't be. It was a really bad one this time, wasn't it?"

Dean turned his head to get a better look at Mikael. "This time?"

"Dean, you might try to hide it when you're awake, but you can't do that in your sleep. You've been having bad dreams since we came back from the mountain."

He had been, but he hadn't thought he'd been that obvious about it. It seemed he'd been less able to cover it up than he'd originally believed. There had been times when he wondered if he'd thrashed or cried out in his sleep. Mikael had never said anything, so Dean had been hoping that the worst he had done was wake up suddenly.

"I'm sorry. I didn't mean to wake you up," Dean said quietly, wishing he could curl in on himself.

"Again, don't be. I just wish you would talk to me."

There it was again, someone wanting him to talk about it. He knew they were only worried about him, and that he wasn't doing as good a job at hiding his sleep problems as he thought. Even if it was Mikael, he still didn't want to talk about it. How could he explain to anyone he just wanted to ride this out until it passed? If he did, it would just open up an opportunity for them to push him to talk more. It would be like admitting something was wrong in the first place, when all he wanted to do was get past it.

"It was just a bad dream, Mikael. Thankfully not a prophetic one." God, he hoped not.

"Hilarious. Anyone ever tell you that you're stubborn?"

Dean smiled at that. "You, at least once or twice a week."

"Because it's true."

Dean rolled around to face Mikael, giving him a small kiss on the end of the nose, "I'm going to take a quick shower. Worked up a little bit of a sweat and I know I stink."

"Good idea."

Dean's frown fell away when he saw Mikael getting up as well. "You don't have to keep me company."

"I didn't shower after getting home. I probably stink, too."

"You smell good to me."

Mikael took Dean's hand and led him to the bathroom. "Been sniffing me again?"

Standing by the shower, Dean reached past Mikael to get the water flowing. "It's kind of hard not to smell you when you're that close. Come to think of it, I've never actually known you to smell bad, ever. Even if you've been working out in the sun all day, you always just smell more like you. Lord, is that another werewolf perk?"

Mikael pulled his shirt over his head, shoving the lounge pants that had been resting nicely on his hips down to the floor. He wasn't putting on a performance, but Dean was appreciating the impromptu strip show all the same. It was hard to think about cold, bloody dreams when you had a hot, flesh and blood man with a body like Mikael's stripping in front of you.

"Gonna stand there and stare at me or you gonna get in with me?"

Shaking himself, Dean wiggled out of his own clothes and threw them on top of Mikael's. Coming here during the summers, the two bathrooms of the farm house had always been equipped with standard tubs and shower heads. At some point after Dean had stopped coming, his grandfather had a stand-in shower installed in the main bedroom's bathroom. It had the wonderful effect of allowing both of them to fit in there without having to worry about slipping in a curved tub. With the addition of a large shower head Dean had installed for the both of them to enjoy, Dean was plenty happy with the shower arrangement most days.

The brief spark of heat he had seen in Mikael's gaze was gone by the time they had both soaked themselves under the warm spray. He was trying to hide it, but Mikael was looking Dean over again, checking to see if Dean was really okay. Dean hoped he wasn't looking like he was trying to shake off the remnants of the dream.

"C'mere," Mikael mumbled, reaching out to pull Dean in closer. Dean felt himself melt into the strength of Mikael's arms, turning around so his back was pressed to his mate's chest. He loved having Mikael hold him, no matter what position they were in. But this position allowed him to lean forward as Mikael squeezed some shampoo into his hand and rubbed it into Dean's hair. His fingers massaged deep into Dean's scalp, sending tingling jolts through his body.

"Is this the aftercare moment after a nightmare?"

"Shh."

Dean let Mikael rinse his hair clean, shivering as the warm water ran down the air cooled patch of skin on his neck. Mikael's lips found the exact same spot, kissing softly as he pulled Dean into him once again. Dean hummed happily, feeling the last remnants of his dream drain from him as Mikael's hand rubbed a path back and forth over his stomach. The other hand fumbled with the bottle of body wash, just managing to squeeze out a healthy sized dollop.

His scalp wasn't the only thing that was getting a massage. Mikael's doting fingers swept over his body, rubbing at tight muscles. Dean groaned when his fingertips found the knot of muscles in his lower back. Mikael's fingers lingered there, no longer cleaning Dean but letting his strength knead away at the stiffness.

"I've got you," Mikael told him, one hand holding onto Dean when his knees weakened, threatening to spill him to the floor. It had been ages since anyone had given him a massage. The last one had been an ex who hadn't used nearly the strength that Mikael was using. The man's fingers were digging deep, finding each knot in his back and shoulders. It was painful, feeling his grip working the muscles, but God did it feel good.

"I promise," Mikael added, still holding tight to Dean's waist.

"I know, I know," Dean gasped, fighting to press back against Mikael. He was a wall of muscle behind him, radiating both warmth and strength. Just about every part of Mikael was pressed against him, and Dean groaned again when he felt Mikael's long, thick cock against his back. He wasn't completely hard, but it was enough to stir Dean's desire.

"Enjoying yourself?" Dean asked, grinning around a grimace as Mikael's fingers dug into another knot.

"Wasn't trying to, but you're making some really... familiar noises," Mikael grunted, his voice sounding strained.

Not one to pass up an opportunity when it came his way, Dean reached behind him to wrap his fingers around Mikael's cock. Mikael's hips jerked, pressing his rapidly hardening erection into Dean's grip. The hands that had been focused on massaging him stuttered, finally holding onto Dean in earnest now. Mikael pushed his hips forward, cock sliding between Dean's slick fingers and up along the crack of his ass.

"You just can't behave, can you?" Mikael asked, trying to sound annoyed and failing totally.

"You feel too good," Dean told him, leaning back once more as Mikael returned the favor, gripping hold of Dean's cock.

Dean moaned as Mikael's grip slid slowly along his length, his fingers stopping briefly to play gently with the head. The urgency in his hold told Dean they probably weren't going to make it to the bedroom before this was over. It wasn't helped by the fact that Mikael's other hand was pushing between their bodies. Water wasn't enough to get Mikael's cock into him, but it was enough for something considerably smaller.

He gasped as Mikael's finger pushed past the ring of muscles in his ass. His hand thrashed out, smacking into the nearby shelf in the shower and holding on tight. His knees wobbled slightly as he felt Mikael's finger slide as deep as it could inside him. His hand never stopped the slow pumping of Dean's cock, drawing a whimper from him.

"Shit," Dean swore, forced to use his other hand to grip onto Mikael's thigh to hold himself up.

"Still got you," Mikael reminded him, the arm around one side of his waist squeezing his hip to prove his point. Dean was barely holding himself up with his own strength, his hold on the shelf and Mikael's thigh only just keeping him upright. There was no way he was going to last like this, not with Mikael stroking him while slipping his finger inside his ass repeatedly. There was a reason he kept his hands off himself when Mikael was inside of him. His orgasm had always been right around the corner when someone was inside of him, especially if it was Mikael.

"Mikael," Dean gasped, trying to wriggle away from him. It felt too damn good and he didn't want it to end just yet. Mikael was still pressing against his back, cock sandwiched between their bodies. His legs already felt weak enough as it was, he didn't want to end up a slumped mess on the floor of the shower.

Not surprisingly, Mikael never hesitated, not once, as he drew Dean closer to his orgasm. Dean's body tightened, instinct pressing him back into Mikael for support. His cry echoed around the bathroom, hips pushing forward as he came. His muscles tightened to the point that he could feel Mikael's finger curled within him. Pleasure washed through him, wiping his mind clean as his cock spilled itself over the floor of the shower.

True to his word, Mikael held Dean up as his body gave in to post-orgasm weakness. The arm around his waist held him up long enough for Mikael to slide his finger free and brace Dean's shoulders. Dean's breathing was ragged, legs still shaking as he tried to make sense of the world again. Not once did he question Mikael's strength as he got his breathing under control, letting himself slump happily against his mate's chest.

After a few minutes of breathing evenly, Dean nodded. "I think I can stand up now."

Mikael laughed. "You sure?"

Dean turned around, running his hands up along the muscles and hair of Mikael's chest. His eyes drifted down to Mikael's half-hard cock still trapped between them. Dean was plenty satisfied, but there was no way he was going to leave Mikael like that. Not in the entire course of their relationship had only one of them gotten off, and Dean wasn't about to let it happen now.

Moving carefully, Dean let himself sink down into a crouch in front of Mikael, using his hands on Mikael's hips to steady himself. Mikael was quickly getting hard again, his eagerness flashing in his eyes as he intently watched Dean position himself. Dean's eyes moved up, locking on Mikael's as he leaned forward and took the head of his cock into his mouth.

Mikael's eyes slid half shut as Dean slid his mouth forward with a moan which vibrated along the length of Mikael's cock. It took no time at all for Mikael to harden to his considerable length. Without their special oil on hand, Dean's throat was never going to be able to take more than half of Mikael's cock into it. But that didn't mean Dean didn't give it his best as he slid Mikael's cock between his lips.

Dean never moved his hands from Mikael's hips, not even as his mate pressed his hand to the back of Dean's head. This was the one time that Mikael never asserted himself, not unless they had used the numbing oil anyway. His fingers wrapped themselves in Dean's hair, a low moan rumbling from deep within his chest. There was a dull thump as Mikael leaned back, his shoulders hitting one of the solid walls of the shower. His eyes never left Dean's face, watching raptly as Dean tried to take him even deeper.

Sex with Mikael rarely involved a lot of oral action. Most of it consisted of their customary rush to penetration, the rutting that followed was usually rough and to the point. Dean never thought he would be the type to be okay without a whole lot of foreplay, but it was easy with Mikael. It made the moments when he could feel the thick shaft sliding into his mouth all the better. Mikael was prone to going gentle and compliant when Dean blew him, happy to just watch and let it happen.

That suited Dean just fine. Even with the water occasionally splashing up into his face, he never hesitated as he slid up and down. He traced the underside of Mikael's cock, the taste of him bitter yet sweet on his tongue as he slid forward once more. Mikael's deep moans were quickly becoming the kind of near growling that ran straight to Dean's core.

Mikael's fingers tightened in his hair, pulling him a little closer. His cock seemed to swell in Dean's mouth as he came. Cum splashed across Dean's tongue, and he swallowed eagerly. Mikael's growl as his hips jerked drew a moan from Dean as another splash lit across his tongue. He sucked eagerly, trying to catch every drop that came from Mikael.

Pain flared for the briefest moment as Mikael used the hand in Dean's hair to pull him off his cock. Dean gasped for a second as he was pulled upward, Mikael's mouth suddenly crushed against his own. The taste of his mate was still on Dean's tongue as Mikael kissed him, slow and deep, wrapping his arms around him, holding him tight as they both savored the kiss.

When the kiss finally broke, Dean blinked slowly up at Mikael. "I love you."

Mikael ran a thumb over Dean's lower lip, eyes practically glowing. "And I you."

"I think I'm ready to go to sleep now. Hold me as I sleep?"

"Always."

CHAPTER 4

"Feels like it's been forever since we were able to do this."

Dean nodded slowly, feeling lazy as they sprawled on the couch together. It was one of those summer days that was warm, but not warm enough to justify keeping the AC on. The happy compromise involved them laying out on the couch with nothing on. It was the first day they'd had some downtime where neither of them had a long list of things to do or without someone else hanging around.

"I feel very lazy right now," Dean admitted, bathing in the warmth of the room and Mikael's body. They would eventually have to get up before they stuck to one another, but Dean was too comfortable to even consider moving before then.

"You're just saying that because your legs don't wanna work right."

Dean chuckled. "True. That's very modest of you, by the way."

"Babe, no one moans the way you moan if they don't

end up having trouble walking afterward. You make me feel like a sex god or something."

Dean ran a hand up one of Mikael's calves. "Maybe you are or were in another life."

"Glad I can satisfy."

They both knew it was far more than just being satisfied. As Mikael had said, Dean wasn't much for holding himself back vocally. It wasn't that he was putting on a show, or simply doing it to make Mikael feel better. The sex between them was, hands down, the best Dean had ever had. There was no way he was going to restrain the noises if he didn't have good reason to. Really, he was more surprised he even had the strength to do that much when Mikael was inside of him.

"Is this going to be one of those days where we do nothing but nap, cuddle, and fuck?" Dean asked, prodding Mikael's side with a toe.

"I mean, we haven't had one of those in a while. Would that be so bad?"

Dean laughed. "Aren't couples supposed to experience a drop in their sex drive after a year, or something? By the end of the season, we'll have been together for a year, and we're still having sex like it's the first month."

"Is this the part where I tell you that werewolves have a high sex drive?"

"I think you mentioned that before, but I'm not a werewolf."

"Animal magnetism?"

"Oh my god."

"Fine, maybe you're just a horndog."

Dean yanked out the pillow he was resting on and threw it at Mikael. "Ass."

Mikael caught the pillow with a laugh. "I'm not wrong, am I?"

"Don't hear you complaining."

"Oh, far from it."

Dean stuck his tongue out, not caring that it was childish. If he were honest, it really could be any of the above. He had been attracted to the few people he had dated before, and the people he had slept with. His attraction to all his previous partners paled in comparison to how he felt about Mikael. It didn't matter how many times they had sex. As soon as Mikael touched him, it always felt like the first time. The only difference was that the touch wasn't exciting because it was new, but because it was well-known, exhilarating in its familiarity. There was a security in being held, grabbed, kissed, and even manhandled by Mikael that he had known nowhere else.

"You're doing that thinking thing again."

Dean jerked, yanked from his happy thoughts. "Thinking about this amazing guy I've got in my life. Kinda makes me starry-eyed sometimes."

"Aren't we feeling soft-hearted today?"

It was said with a grin, and Dean poked him with his toe one more time for extra emphasis. He wouldn't say that he was necessarily sleeping any better. The nightmares were still going to happen. He knew that, and there wasn't much he could do about it except wait it out. But after the night before, he had managed to sleep peacefully. Mikael had stayed curled around him throughout the rest of the night, with Dean waking up next to him in the morning.

The front door crashed open, banging against the wall as someone barreled into the hallway with a shout. Dean rolled off the couch with a startled yelp, trying to get out of sight of whatever had just forced its way into his home.

Mikael however, had stood up, muscles bunching as he prepared himself for a fight. A strong whiff of Mikael's scent hit Dean, and he realized that Mikael was getting ready to go full-on wolf.

"Dante?"

Mikael's annoyed question hung in the air as Dean pushed himself up off of the floor. Sure enough, the grumpy looking werewolf stood in the doorway to the living room. Dean didn't know who was more startled, them or Dante. The expert tracker was looking stunned as his eyes flashed between the two of them.

"Holy shit," Dante barked. "Why the fuck aren't you wearing any clothes?"

Dean scoffed. "You help yourself through the front door of our house and demand to know why we aren't wearing any clothes?"

Dante sniffed the air, wrinkling his nose. "Oh shit, tell me I didn't interrupt you guys in the middle of screwing or something. It reeks of sex and lube in here."

Sighing, Dean began searching for their clothing. "We were between rounds, but thanks for asking."

Dante gave Mikael a pained expression, "Mikael, man. Pants?"

Dean tossed them to Mikael, who didn't move except to catch the pants. Dante was doing his best to maintain eye contact with Mikael. Dean had thought werewolves weren't all that shy about nudity, but it seemed that wasn't a universal mindset. Dante looked about as uncomfortable as it got as he tried to avoid looking too far below their shoulders.

Dante turned away. "Seriously, is this what you guys do all day? Sit around without clothes on and hump like bunnies?"

"We were enjoying having no one over and a day completely to ourselves," Dean griped as he yanked his underwear and shorts on.

"Right up until a certain pack member decided to almost break down our door," Mikael added, still not having put any clothing on, or even bothering to cover himself in the slightest. Dean suspected he was doing it on purpose to embarrass Dante even more. That, or it was some weird werewolf dominance thing. He hadn't seen much of that from his mate before, but anything was possible. And it was the first time someone had so completely interrupted them in the midst of an intimate and vulnerable moment.

"Mikael. Look I'm sorry man, but I wasn't thinking. I came here to tell you, Lucille is awake."

Dean jerked upright, spinning to face Dante. "Are you serious?"

Mikael was instantly fighting to get his pants on. "When?"

Dante peaked over his shoulder, seeing that they were decent now, he turned to face them. "Last night. They wanted to make sure she was alright before they sent word out. But she's awake, talking and everything."

"How is she?" Dean asked as he wrestled his shirt on.

"Weak, but she was a little stronger before I left than she was last night. She even took a nap and woke up a few hours later. But they're wanting you guys to come back."

Mikael was already forcing his shoes on. "Of course I'm coming back."

Dean hesitated, looking out the front window toward the driveway. If this had been winter or even the beginning of spring, he would have been out the door before Mikael. Now though, with the farm in full swing and needing a lot of care, he hesitated.

"Dean?"

Dean turned to Mikael with a grimace. "I'm going to have to call the Williams'. Maybe even call one of the locals to come and help them."

Dante snorted. "Seriously, you're worried about that? Just come back with us."

Dean frowned. "Last I checked, I'm helping provide food to the pack with this farm, Dante. And I'm not going to leave the animals to fend for themselves. I don't mind having Mr. Williams take care of the animals, but I'd really prefer to have someone here to help him with the fields. I know he did it before, but there's more out there than last year."

"I understand Dean. You don't have to explain," Mikael assured him.

"Okay, but you need to go. You two can get there on four legs faster than if you drove anyway. I'll drive the truck out and meet you guys there once I get something set up."

Mikael nodded, glancing down at the rest of his clothes. "Guess I should throw these in a bag instead, then."

Dante jabbed a thumb over his shoulder at a small bag on his back. "Just throw them in with mine. Come on, she's asking about you."

Dean hesitated, not knowing if this was the right time. "Does she...remember anything?"

Dante shrugged. "I don't know if they asked her. I wasn't around when they did."

He didn't have anything to say to that, growing quiet as the two werewolves talked quietly. Mikael looked up after a moment, frowning at Dean. Mikael motioned Dante out with the promise that he would follow. Once they heard him close the door and thump down the steps of the porch, Mikael moved closer to him.

"What's wrong?" Mikael asked.

"Nothing that can't wait," Dean replied, thinking of the messenger tube they had found on Lucille. It was safely stowed away back at the Grove, under Matalina's safe keeping. Dean hadn't wanted that thing anywhere near where he lived after what had happened in the mountain. He remembered all too clearly how Damian had spoken of what should have been a pack of six tubes. Dean couldn't be certain that they were even the same tubes. But if he was right, and they were the same thing, it meant that Damian had only had four, the fifth had somehow ended up with Lucille.

Where was the sixth?

"You sure?"

Dean could see Mikael was concerned, but he also wanted to already be halfway across the fields and into the woods. Dean hadn't had siblings of his own, but he could understand the feeling. If it was Mikael that had just woken up after over half a year of being in a coma, Dean wouldn't have stood around this long to wait to see him. It was only Mikael's need to make sure Dean was okay that was keeping him here.

"Go. Shouldn't take me long to head out," Dean told him, leaning up to kiss him quickly and pat his butt.

Mikael returned the kiss before turning and hurrying out of the house. Dean watched them through the front window. He caught the last few seconds of their transition into their wolf forms. The last traces of Mikael's human skin disappeared behind a patch of fur as he shook himself off. The beautiful predator that was his mate pawed at the ground, eyeing the dark wolf that was Dante. And just like that, they were gone, speeding off toward the forest's edge.

He watched the tree line for a moment, chewing his

bottom lip. Before he could sink too deeply into his thoughts, he pushed away from the window to find his phone. Service might be non-existent within the Grove, but at least he had it while at home. He found the phone in between the cushions of the couch and dug it out to dial the Williams' and explain the situation.

"Again?" Mr. Williams asked quietly.

"I'm sorry, Mr. Williams. I know you're busy with your own things, and there's more to do here than there was last year. I was kind of hoping you knew some local kids who might need the work, and could come out here and help."

"I ain't *that* old, Dean."

Dean sighed, having expected this. "I didn't say that. But I think your wife would kill us both if you were over here all day long, slaving away on *my* farm."

"Ah," Mr. Williams grunted. "You might be right about that one. I know a couple of boys from down the way who could use the work."

"Alright, I'll leave plenty of money in my grandfather's chest for you to pay them with."

"How long this time?"

Dean hesitated. "Uh, should only be a few days. It's a family thing going on, and I want to be there with Mikael."

"Uh huh, you've said 'only a few days' before Dean," Mr. Williams chuckled. "I know what that means. I just hope you don't come back a couple of weeks later, looking worse than you do now."

"Mr. Williams, please."

"I said I'd do it, and I'll do it."

"I'll leave the key to the chest on the kitchen table for you. Feel free to take some and buy yourself something nice."

Mr. Williams snorted before ending the call, leaving

Dean to set his phone down with a worried frown. He was only going out to see Lucille and make sure she was okay. It was simply a matter of visiting the people who were essentially his in-laws. Everything had calmed down since Damian had died, there wasn't a threat hovering over the Grove anymore.

So why did he feel like this was only the eye of the storm?

CHAPTER 5

The welcoming party was small when he pulled into the Grove in Mikael's truck. Matalina and Apollo stood a safe distance away from the small patch of land used to park the few vehicles the pack owned. Dean hadn't seen anyone but Mikael drive before, but none of the other cars looked neglected or unused. He imagined they must be used at some point and he wondered who did the driving around here.

By the time he stepped out of the truck onto the grass, Matalina was waiting for him. The last time he had seen her, she'd been looking as tired as everyone was now saying he did. She still looked tired, but some of her warmth had returned. Lucille's awakening had brought some of the old lightness back to her step as she came forward to wrap him up in a hug.

"We didn't know if you were going to make it today," she said in greeting, beaming the whole time.

Apollo seemed happier too, stepping forward to hug Dean as well. Dean smiled at the both of them, basking in their affection. It was so strange to have all these people care so much about him. It had been so long since he had something like this. Everything, from the affection to the butting heads, was like having a family all over again. It was just one more thing for him to hold onto whenever his thoughts returned to the dark beneath the ground.

"Matalina, you look good," Dean told her as she took his hand in hers.

"I believe you mean tired but thank you, Dean. I have hoped that this day would come. I have never felt more awake than I do right now. My daughter has been returned to me."

"How is she?" he asked.

"She is still quite weak. We did what we could while she was asleep to keep atrophy at bay, but there was only so much we could do. We are a resilient species and we heal quite quickly. Still, it will take some time before she gets back to her old state again. Yet, she is young and strong-willed. I know she will return to her former self one day soon. For now, she rests when she can, which frightens us each time she closes her eyes. She opens her eyes every time, though."

"Has she said anything?"

Matalina shook her head. "Not anything important, if that is what you mean. Mostly it has been asking about what she has missed. For all her eccentricities, she is a strong woman and has been undaunted by her predicament. She tries to question us as much as she can. She's asked to speak to you, when she's awake again."

Dean nodded, not sure what she could want with him. "Of course."

She clasped her hands together. "I will return to her bedside then. I know she is out of danger now, however I cannot help but want to be by her side. Come in when you are ready."

Dean watched her walk off, definitely looking a little lighter in her step than she had before. Actually, the entire the Grove seemed a little lighter. He hadn't actually noticed the heavy atmosphere before, but with it gone, he definitely noticed its absence. Everyone in the Grove seemed to be out today, milling about and chatting happily. It was clear the news of Lucille's awakening had been met with a great deal of joy.

"It's nice to see everyone happy again. Even you, Apollo," Dean punched the quiet werewolf's shoulder playfully.

"After everything that happened, it is nice to have some truly good news," Apollo murmured quietly, smiling softly down at Dean.

Dean took Apollo's arm in his and began to walk toward the main house. "Agreed. Other than this, how have you been, Apollo? Haven't seen you since the last time I was here."

"Father has kept me busy."

"Scouting?"

"Yes, and working with the trackers to help with any search and rescue that needs to be done. The border fighting between packs is causing a lot of chaos."

"Let me guess. Been paired with up Dante, huh?"

Apollo shrugged. "We work well together."

"Hey, if it works, it works. I know you must be happy to see him again after he spent so long away."

"It has been nice to have my friend around again."

"Friend? What happened to 'cousin?' Not a term you use anymore?"

Apollo shrugged again, his only answer was an unreadable stare. Dean stared back, raising a brow in question, but receiving no further answer in return. Apollo was a hard person to read, and if he didn't want to share something, he was quite skilled at concealing it. Dean was only getting that blank look in return, and not for the first time, he wondered what was going on in Apollo's head.

"Oh, ya did show up," Dante's loud voice cut through the silent questioning, catching both Apollo and Dean's attention.

Mikael and Dante stood outside the door to the main house, grinning at the two of them. Apollo quickly pulled his arm free from Dean's grip, making Dean looked sideways at him, but he simply got a little shake of Apollo's head in return. When Dean looked at the two men approaching them, he saw that Dante was also giving Apollo a strange look. It wasn't quite a frown and if Dean were to take a guess he'd say it was a look of concern and confusion.

"Got everything taken care of?" Mikael asked when he was close enough. He too wasn't immune to the brightening effect that Lucille's awakening had on everyone. Mikael was practically grinning from ear to ear as he stood before Dean.

"Yeah, wasn't a big deal. Even got Mr. Williams to agree to getting some teenagers out there to help him."

"Wasn't sure if you would be able to. Seems like the stubborn type."

Dean shrugged. "All I had to do was mention how mad Mrs. Williams would be if he was out there all the time and he warmed up to the idea."

Mikael laughed. "That would do it."

Dean smiled at the warm sound of Mikael's laugh. "I take it you got to talk to her?"

"Yeah, she was awake when I showed up."

"He barely had his clothes on before he burst into the room," Dante informed Dean.

Mikael didn't look at all ashamed. "We talked for a little while before she fell asleep again. You'd think, given she's been sleeping for over half a year, she would have had enough of it. But I guess it's just part of the healing process. Silun says she probably won't be sleeping like this for very long; it's just her body having to adjust to moving around again."

"Wow. He's really coming into his own as the resident medical expert, huh?" Dean asked, proud of the shaman in training. Silun doubted himself when it came to his abilities as a shaman, as a werewolf, and as a person. He sure as hell didn't doubt himself when it came to taking care of wounded people, though. The seemingly shy and awkward werewolf had shouted down the intimidating looking Dante when Apollo had been badly injured months ago. It was good to hear that he was finding a niche he felt comfortable in.

"Kid's something else," Dante commented. "Couldn't get him to hardly talk to me when he first came here. Now he won't shut up."

Thinking of what he had learned about Silun's feelings for Dante, he frowned at the tracker. "You better be nice to him Dante. I mean it."

"Aww, I ain't gonna be mean to a kid. Gimme a break Dean, geez."

Mikael nudged Dean. "You wanna see if she's awake? She asked to speak to you earlier when I spoke to her. That was a couple of hours ago."

Dean nodded. "Your mom said the same thing, and yeah, if she's up to it."

Dante snorted, following Dean and Mikael only after Apollo trailed after them first. "You kidding me? When she found out about everything that happened while she was out cold, she sounded so disappointed that she missed all of it. I think she was waiting for you to pull some shit before all of this, and then she finds out you only pulled some shit when she was unconscious."

Pulled some shit? That was an interesting way of looking at it, though Dean found himself agreeing with the odd statement. There wasn't really a better way to describe the events of the past few months. Dean had spent his time rushing from one disaster and headlong into another. He almost wished he had been the one who had slept through it all.

As they walked through the main house back to the room where they had been looking after Lucille, Dean realized he hadn't seen Samuel. It was possible that the alpha was with Lucille, but he thought it was strange that no one had mentioned him even in passing. If anything, he would have expected the older man to be in his usual spot in the main room.

"Your dad with Lucille?"

"No, he had to go out to the borders earlier this afternoon. Scouts found something they said he needed to go see personally."

"Really?" Dean asked, sounding surprised. For all of Samuel's bluster and seemingly invincible status, the alpha had been as torn up about Lucille's condition as the rest of them. For him to leave only a day after she woke up was strange. That, and Dean didn't think he had ever heard of Samuel leaving the Grove itself. The answer came when he looked at Mikael, who had probably arrived shortly before Samuel had left. Samuel's absence meant that, for now, Mikael was the one in charge. Dean was betting that nothing had directly been said, just understood. It had been a long time coming, but Samuel seemed to finally have faith in his chosen heir.

Mikael opened the door leading to the back rooms. "Yeah. One of the scouts showed up, had a private meeting with him and then he was gone. Barely said more than that to me before he left."

Dean was hoping it wasn't another impending disaster ready to drop in their laps. The scattered fighting from the dissolved pack Damian had formed was enough. The few months since Damian's death had been the most peaceful Dean had since moving to his farm. Perhaps it was only him jumping at shadows, but he couldn't shake the feeling that trouble was waiting just around the corner.

As they stepped into Lucille's room, Dean's eyes were drawn to the bed against the far wall. The small woman was sitting upright, a handful of pillows stacked behind her. Her almost yellow eyes turned to him as he entered. She was the one member of the family he had, so far, had very little to do with, and he still wasn't sure where they stood. The last time they had really talked, she had been strange and distant with him. Her face was as unreadable as Matalina's when the Alpha Bitch chose to be, though it was more sharply defined, like Samuel's.

"And our troublemaker returns as a savior," Lucille said in greeting, her voice harsh sounding from disuse.

"Hi Lucille," Dean replied awkwardly, remembering that they hadn't really developed a rapport before all this happened. She was looking at him now in the same way she'd done when they first met, with an unnerving distant interest. It made him feel a bit like a bug under a magnifying glass. It did nothing for his nerves, and he shifted uneasily as Mikael and Dante slipped quietly to another corner of the room.

"How are you feeling?" he asked after a prolonged silence.

"Ironically, I am tired, but that will pass. Before sleep finds its way to me once more, I wish to speak with you a bit. If you are willing, that is."

"Uh, sure," he glanced around, seeing that the only chair in the room that wasn't occupied by someone or something was the one nearest her bed. Still feeling a little uncomfortable, he sat down. She looked at him for a moment, her eyes searching his face but saying nothing. He couldn't tell if she was making up her mind about him in that moment, or if she was simply fighting with an understandably foggy mind to try to find the question she wanted to ask.

"I have heard a few stories from my family. About the events I missed over the last few months. Like facets of a gem, I have seen different sides of these events. I have tried to stay awake long enough to hear them all, but I have yet to hear yours. You, who have been at the center of everything, or at least near enough to it all. So please, would you be so kind as to tell me your side of events?"

Even beneath the tiredness, he could hear the eager curiosity in her voice. It was the inquisitive nature he had heard attributed to her many times by many people. She had certainly missed quite a few significant events. For someone who liked to know everything that was happening, he imagined it was immensely frustrating for her to have missed so much. He didn't know what she would gain from his side of the story, but he didn't see much harm in telling her.

Taking a deep breath, he began his story from the point she had been found by the scouts. Detailing the break-in at the warehouse by Apollo and him, and his subsequent capture. His learning about Damian's plan and then the full scope of the man's psychotic aims after he had been rescued. Even as he moved on to telling of his dream and how it lead to the huge effort to rescue the shamans, he was careful about what he said. He had no problem detailing their travels, and the fights they had to endure to survive. He couldn't bring himself to describe the fear and pain he felt about his time as a prisoner of Damian's pack, the sheer horror of his fight with Scar, or his despair at both killing Damian and having to leave the shamans behind to die.

He would give her credit; she was an excellent listener. Not once did he feel that she wasn't listening or had become lost in her own thoughts. She never interrupted him as he spoke, simply nodding silently as he told his tale. It took longer than he thought it would, and he felt drained when he had finally finished.

For the longest time she said nothing, still staring at Dean long after he had grown silent. The feeling of being under a microscope returned to him. He had faced down multiple werewolves, faced death and torture, but he couldn't remember feeling quite as uncomfortable as he did under her penetrating stare. It was as if she could see into his mind, and was rooting through each thought and memory in there, including the ones he hadn't told.

"And your abilities?" she finally asked.

"I'm...getting there. I can communicate with just about any plant now, and I have some measure of control over them if I want it. Still don't know how I managed to get super strong a couple of times, but if I figured out how to talk to plants, I can figure that out eventually."

"Could it have been influenced by tapping into the power of the mountain?"

He thought about that for a moment before shaking his

head. "No, I don't think so. Because I was doing it before we even reached the mountain. It has to be something else."

"Tapping into the strength of the earth?"

"Something like that."

She nodded slowly. "You may just be onto something with that. But I can see a question in your eyes. Ask it."

"Tell me about the tube, Lucille."

At that, she sighed, nodding her head again as if she had expected the question. "Yes, the tube. If you are going to ask what was in it, I can't tell you. But from the sounds of it, you already suspect what it held."

"A crystal."

"While I was out delivering messages, I was also collecting information. In the course of my travels I got close to the original home of Damian's pack. Among his things, I discovered a collection, an assortment of objects I believe were once owned by the shaman, Nox. I do remember the object Damian spoke to you of. Five tubes, bound together with an empty space for another that was nowhere to be seen with the rest. I could only take the one tube before having to leave. I had every intention of returning here with all that I had learned, and I didn't wish to be caught."

"What else did you find?"

"It doesn't matter. It's all useless to us now that he is dead and his collected packs have scurried back to their corners or are still fighting one another. I do not know what happened to the notes and messages I took with me, or what led me to conceal the tube on my person. I don't even know what happened after I opened the tube, if that's actually what I did."

"Do you remember when this was?"

At that, she smiled softly. "Almost a month before I was found. So either there is a large gap in my memory of adventures I missed, or I opened it earlier than that and...something happened."

"Something?"

"You, Apollo, and Silun all described the same strange effects of a fully-grown crystal. Who is to say exactly what happened when I opened that tube? However, I do find it interesting that it was Damian's pack that inevitably found me. That's a strange coincidence."

"Do you think he knew you had it and deliberately let you keep it when he dumped you back in our territory?"

"I cannot say. To what end?"

Dean had no immediate answer to that question. Damian had been a master of appearing to do one thing while doing something entirely different. Dean thought the former alpha would have considered it a slow day if he didn't have at least one or two other plans concealed behind the first two. The werewolf had been the most conniving and manipulative person Dean had ever known. He had also been intelligent and strong-willed, enough to follow through on his ingenious plans. If he hadn't been blinded by his arrogance and self-serving ambition, he might have been an asset to all werewolves, or he might at least have been still alive.

"I don't know. Was there anything in there about where they came from? The tubes?"

She shook her head. "Not that I can remember. Most of what I saw there were Nox's own notes and what appeared to be a journal. I had thought to grab it as well, but I was pressed for time as it was. I apologize, Dean. That is all I can tell you."

Dean smiled. "It's alright, Lucille. It's not like I was expecting anything to be easy."

"Few things are," she replied with a wan smile. "But I

think I need to rest some more. It's frustrating how easily I grow tired, and from something as simple as talking, no less."

He rose as she settled herself back into the pillows behind her. When he turned, he saw Mikael and Dante looking at him intently. Mikael looked a little sad, but resigned. Dante simply looked amused, smirking up at him.

"Time to solve a mystery?" Dante asked casually, drumming his fingers lightly on the table before him.

His tendency to give away his thoughts when he was thinking hard already told them what was running through his mind. He'd already seen what was possible from a few crystals being in the wrong hands. Together, they had become several hundred times larger than they were individually. He didn't know what the power within them could be used for, but if Nox's abilities were any indication, it was dangerous.

There was still an unaccounted for tube out there, with one of those crystals in it. One that was separated from the rest and had been missing for who knew how long. Four of them had grown rapidly in the course of couple of months. He didn't know if there were other ways to make them grow stronger, only that using shamans had been Damian's method of choice. He had to find that other crystal, or at least learn more about them.

The trick would be to do that without it becoming another disastrous adventure.

CHAPTER 6

"Why does he have that look in his eye? What did Lucille tell him?"

Dean sighed as he looked at Katarina in exasperation. She sounded as amused as Dante had looked. She had approached the three of them as they stepped out of the main house. His mind had still been going over everything he had learned from Lucille, and it must have shown on his face.

"She told him about finding the tube," Mikael offered freely, now frowning at Dean.

"Uh huh, and what crazy place are you planning on dragging us off to this time?" she asked, not sounding bothered by the idea in the slightest.

"Really guys? I'm not plotting our next big adventure here."

"Uh huh," Dante said skeptically. "You've got that look you get."

"I don't have a look!"

Dante snorted. "Yeah, you do. It's the look you got when we were getting ready to leave for the mountain. And the one you had on your face when you went and got yourself caught by Damian. It's your 'I'm totally about to do something fucking insane' face."

"Even if that were true, which it's not!" Dean insisted, "I wouldn't know where to even start. We don't know where that other tube could have even gone. Lucille said she didn't grab any of his notes and I'm sure Damian's stuff has been pilfered by now. Hell, I don't even know where the damn things came from in the first place. I have no place to start, so there's not some 'adventure' I'm planning."

"I believe I can help with that."

Dean turned towards the oddly familiar voice, brow raising at the sight of Eveline, the dark eyed woman from the mountain. Samuel stood behind her with a few of the pack's werewolves beside him. With the exception of Eveline, none of them looked happy to be standing there. Remembering Matalina's reaction to the message Eveline had Dean deliver, he wondered if it was such a good idea for her to be here in the Grove.

"Eveline? What are you doing here?" Dean finally asked.

"I'm here to visit an old friend, and to assure him that I have no intention of carrying on Damian's foolish little war with him," she replied with a knowing glance back toward Samuel. She was met with a hard stare, not that it seemed to bother her in the slightest. From the looks of it, she had been brought here alone and Dean wondered if she had traveled by herself or if she had an escort that had been left at the borders.

"And she insisted that what she had with her was for you," Samuel continued for her.

Dean looked at her suspiciously. "What could you have that I would want?"

She held up what appeared to be pages out of a book, rolled up and bound together with a rubber band. "Something from Damian's possessions."

Mikael stepped forward, reaching his hand out to take the rolled-up papers from her. For a moment, it looked as if she wouldn't let them go. Her gaze moved from Mikael, to Dean, and held there. Her eyes lingered on him, and her fingers eventually uncurled their grip from the papers so that Mikael could take them.

Mikael pulled the rubber band free, unrolling the pages. "And this is the only thing you got?"

She shrugged. "I was lucky to get that much and it's useless to me. But I believe it might just hold the answers you're looking for."

"What is this, a journal?" Mikael asked as he flipped through the papers.

From what Dean could see, it looked almost like a scrapbook. There was certainly plenty of writing covering each page, all seemingly written by the same hand. In places, however, there were scraps of paper taken from somewhere else, torn or cut from their original source and stuck on the pages Mikael held in his hand. The writing on some of those scraps differed from the others, and Dean spotted a few sketches stuck in there as well.

"Do you recognize it?" Dean asked, noticing that Mikael was frowning at the pages.

"I'm pretty sure this is Damian's handwriting," Mikael told him, his fingers tracing the parts of the pages that weren't torn out from somewhere else.

"I'm pretty sure the scraps are from Nox," Eveline told them.

"And how do you know that?" Dante asked from somewhere over Dean's shoulder.

"I did read over it enough to get that much. That man was obsessed with Nox. Everything from where he had been, to what he could do. Obsessed enough that I'm pretty sure they were screwing."

Dean wrinkled his nose, having suspected the same thing when he was back in the mines. Somehow it wasn't comforting that someone else had thought the same thing. If that was true, neither of them had been all that bothered by the idea of sharing. Dean wasn't sure whether Nox harbored any ideas about using Dean's body for pleasure, but he knew that Damian certainly had. He didn't know what disgusted him more, the idea of sleeping with Damian, or sleeping with someone who had willingly slept with Nox.

"Okay, so why would you bring this to me? What makes you think this will help me with anything at all?"

"Please. Damian spoke about you enough that all of us knew you were one of the big prizes for whatever his endgame was. We all knew what you were, and he mentioned more than once that his precious Nox had wanted to get his hands on you. It's not hard to figure out that the three of you were tied to one another somehow."

Mikael crossed his arms across his chest. "That's not an explanation. Why don't you just come right out and say that there was nothing in these pages you could use for yourself and you just wanted an excuse to come here personally instead of sending someone to deliver your message for you?"

"You look like your father, but sound like your mother," Eveline said, continuing to look amused.

Dean reached up to take the pages from Mikael. "Is that true?"

Eveline shrugged. "Partly, but that's my personal business. These pages mean nothing to me, and as you know, we all knew Damian was up to something. He wrote about it a little, but it didn't make much sense to me. We also know you went down there, and probably figured out what he was doing, not that you're going to tell us, are you?"

Dean snorted. "No, I'm not."

She didn't look surprised by his answer. "So yes, the papers are in your hands now because I can't do a damn thing with them. And you know, from what I overheard, you might just find something in there that you can use. If you enjoy him talking about himself and going on about crystals and power."

Dean's pulse jumped at the mention of crystals. He looked down at the pages clenched in his hand and he wondered if this was exactly what he needed. If he were lucky, there might just be some answers in these pages. He hoped that the thick pile of papers in his hand held answers to some of the questions he had. All he needed was to know where he had to start looking, somewhere to start his hunt to find the other crystal, or answers to where they came from in the first place.

Mikael grabbed hold of him and pulled him away from the rest of the group. Dean didn't protest; he only looked at his mate in surprise. Outside of the bedroom, Mikael didn't manhandle him. If he was going to break that rule to drag Dean away from the group, Dean figured it had to be something important. It didn't hurt that Mikael's strained expression never wavered as he pulled Dean far enough away to be out of earshot of the rest.

"Mikael?" Dean asked, looking up at his face with worry.

"Are you actually going to do this?"

He hadn't been expecting that. "Do what?"

Mikael jabbed his hand down at the pages he was still

holding. "Go reading through that bastard's journal. Start digging through his ramblings to maybe find some answers so you can go off on another crazy adventure."

Dean stepped back from the heat in Mikael's voice. "I don't understand why you're so angry."

"You don't? Really? Dean, babe, please. I love you and I love how you are, but your crusades are going to be the death of me. Or worse, the death of you. You almost got yourself seriously hurt going up against my dad, then you almost got killed during the ambush. Then you got yourself kidnapped."

"Got myself kidnapped?" Dean interrupted in annoyance. "I didn't go out there trying to find trouble, Mikael. it's not my fault that maniac decided I was his personal toy!"

"That's not what I'm saying at all, damn it. You just charge off when you get an idea in your head, or you start fighting something, and it always ends up with you almost dying or getting seriously hurt. For fuck's sake Dean, you could have died in that mountain!"

"But I didn't, did I?" Dean fought the urge to step back, hurt at this sudden bout of frustration coming from Mikael.

"That's not the point! You haven't even gotten over everything that's happened in the past year yet and now you want to go charging off after something else?"

"Then what is the point? Because last I checked, you were proud of me because I was willing to fight."

"Dean," Mikael breathed, reaching out to try to take hold of him, but Dean pulled away from his hand, glaring up at him. Not only did he have people asking after him like he was fragile or something, but now he was going to have to deal with Mikael actually treating him like he was?

"Well? Was that a lie, or what?"

Mikael gave up trying to take Dean's hand. "No, it

wasn't a lie. I *am* proud of you. I couldn't have chosen a braver mate. It's something else to see you willing to fight for what you believe in, despite what everyone else might say. But damn it Dean, I'm so terrified of losing you over one of these crusades. You went into that mountain as *you*, but you came out...different."

Dean's jaw tightened. "I really wish everyone would stop treating me like I'm going to break at any time."

"I didn't say you were going to break. But don't act like you're not already under a lot of stress. You aren't sleeping much, and when you do, you're having nightmares that wake you up. Sometimes you just check out of a conversation, with a look on your face that breaks my heart. It's not about you being weak, but you're a person Dean, not a superhero."

Dean followed Mikael's frown down to the pages, as he tucked them close to his body in response. "Fine, but I can handle it. I saw what those crystals could do, and I'm not willing to let one of them just float around somewhere in the world. Hell, there could be more and I might be able to do something about that. They're *dangerous* Mikael, in case you forgot."

"You're not even listening to me, are you? I'm telling you that I'm worried about you, and you just tell me you're going to go charging into yet another situation."

Dean took another step back. "Well, stop being worried. I'm fine Mikael, and the sooner you believe me, the sooner you can get over this."

"Get over this? Are you even listening to yourself? Don't dismiss me Dean. That's not right."

"And neither is treating me like a china doll. So I guess we both get to be wrong, don't we?"

Whirling away on his heels, Dean stomped off before

Mikael could say anything else. The others were still standing huddled together in the distance, now watching Dean. Apollo had joined them at some point, and he was frowning in Dean's direction. Everyone else, save for Eveline and her smirk, was watching in silence as he approached.

"Thank you Eveline, I'll get started on reading through these," Dean told the Alpha Bitch as he joined them.

"It will please me if you find something you can use."

Dean snorted. "No it won't. You just want to see what I'll get up to next is all. You've got the same look on your face that you had when I interrupted your meeting with the other alphas and Damian."

"Do you plan on hitting someone with a lantern?"

Katarina made a choking noise. "Is that what you did to get caught?"

Dean sighed. "No, I stood up and announced my presence. I simply hurried along his long winded monologue by smacking him in the face with the lantern someone had brought in with them."

"Scratching up his pretty face into the bargain," Eveline laughed softly, the sound coming from somewhere deep down inside her.

Samuel cleared his throat from behind her. "Dean, get to work. When you figure something out, come to me and we'll talk. Eveline, you've worn out your welcome. It's time for you to leave."

If she was bothered by his curtness, Eveline didn't show it. If anything, she somehow appeared even more amused as she was swiftly led away. Dean watched her go, wondering if she would be a problem at some point. It was possible he was just being paranoid, but experience had recently taught him not to take his suspicions of other's motives at face value. She might not look as if she was up to something, but he wasn't going to discount it either.

"That's a woman who just wants to stir the shit," Dante huffed beside him.

Dean shrugged, looking down at the pages he was holding, "Maybe. At least she was helpful when doing it. If you'll excuse me, I have some reading to do."

And before Mikael could return to the group, Dean marched off without looking back.

CHAPTER 7

I t wasn't that he expected his announcement to be met with great enthusiasm, but the almost stunned silence hadn't been what he expected either. Considering he had spent the past two days reading over the journal entries, he had expected at least some form of immediate response. Instead, Matalina and Samuel just sat across from him in the open room of the main house, staring at him blankly. The only reaction he received was Mikael's anxious fidgeting in the seat next to him.

"Are you sure?" Matalina finally asked.

Dean nodded, tapping the pages before him. "The answer is in the jungle of Central America, close to the South American border."

"And how can you be sure this will lead you to the crystal?" that was Samuel, sounding wary.

"Damian did most of the work, and it's probably not going to lead to the missing crystal. But it is where Nox found them in the first place."

"He just found them, lying out in the jungle?" Mikael asked, sounding doubtful.

Dean shot him a glare. "No. He didn't just find them lying around under a tree. Far as I can tell, he had some text or legend that he was following. There was a temple, a building, something that he found. There were some hostile locals and that's where he found the set of six tubes that contained the crystals."

"Rather than asking questions, let's save time," Matalina interrupted, gesturing to Dean. "Start from the beginning."

Dean took a deep breath, flipping through the pages to open up the first page he wanted. The scraps on the page had come from Nox's own journal. On them were drawn several glyphs, none of them familiar or similar to any he had seen before. They came from the temple Nox found in the jungle, but even Damian didn't have the translation for them. Dean wondered if Nox had kept the translation secret or hadn't actually known himself.

"Damian had obviously taken some of Nox's notes on the temple he apparently found. I don't think he got all the notes Nox left, though. The guy probably had hiding places for a lot of things, and whatever Damian found was probably what Nox had kept close at hand for studying. He probably meant to get back to it after returning from here. I'm not claiming to be an expert on ancient alphabets, but these don't look familiar to me. I can't check it out here. From what I remember, they're not even remotely similar to the style of the Aztec or Mayan alphabet."

Hurriedly, he flipped back to the pages where Damian had written about Nox's journey. One of the biggest hurdles in getting through Damian's writing was his tendency to use an absurd amount of exposition. He tended to rattle on just as much in his written word as he had done with his verbal speeches. Dean learned quickly that he couldn't skim over it when Damian went on and on about a topic, either. Damian peppered his ramblings with important information, making it easy to miss them if Dean was impatient.

"Here," he opened the pages to a hand drawn map with Nox's scattered handwriting on it.

"Is that Damian's work or Nox's?" Matalina asked, leaning forward on her cushion to try to see the page better.

"Nox's. Damian took out the parts he didn't want to copy, I'm guessing. Once you get over how much he liked to talk, you can figure out the stuff he read but didn't copy down. This was the only map Nox ever made and I think he made it while he was still trying to find the place. And before you ask, it's because it's such a rough map. No real clean lines. That and the map and writing were done at different times. You can tell because of how bold or faded the lines are in places."

"If he only drew the local area, how does that help us to know where to start?" Samuel asked, sounding less hesitant than before.

"That was the tricky part, but thankfully someone around here had a book I could use. Chock full of detailed maps and satellite images of all over the world." Dean's luck might not always work for him, but sometimes it came through when he needed it.

"Who?" Mikael asked, now eyeing the large book under the sheets of paper.

"Dante, I think he's a closet nerd. Combing over the maps took me the better part of yesterday. There wasn't a lot to go on to give me an idea of where to start, other than it was in Central America, but closer to South America. I narrowed it down to places that wouldn't be near any cities or towns. Figured if it was, it would have been found and mentioned in some magazine or book. Since you only hear about the Mayans and Aztecs in that area, I thought it was safe to assume it wasn't part of anything anyone knew about."

Dean opened up the book of maps to the picture he was looking for. "It's here. The map that Nox drew doesn't have accurate measurements obviously, but when you take account of the physical landmarks he noted down they match the map. The river he drew isn't nearly as close as it looks, and the oddly shaped hills or mountains are actually closer than they look on his map."

When Samuel motioned him closer, Dean got up and brought both the drawn map and detailed picture from the book with him. Matalina leaned in close to Samuel, and they both looked over the two images. Dean returned to his own cushion, feeling a sense of elation and accomplishment. Once he had returned to Mikael's cabin, he had spent almost all of his time pouring over the information in Damian's journal. This was a mystery he could sink his teeth into and he felt more confident in the results of this research than he had in his vision that sparked the last adventure.

"Well, you have me convinced that you found where Nox had gone," Samuel began slowly, handing the page and picture over to Matalina.

"But?" Dean asked.

"What makes you think this is going to help you in searching for this missing crystal?"

"This is where Nox found them. He had plans for those crystals and probably knew more about them than Damian did. I'm betting the bastard even had a good idea what the glyphs he copied meant. This is where the crystals came from, maybe even where they were made. If I can learn what Nox discovered there, I might be able to figure out exactly what they do and how they work. If I know that, I can figure out who would want that missing crystal and what they could do with it. Hell, there might be even more of them out there in the world, meaning I would need all the information I can get to try and hunt them down and destroy them."

Samuel raised an eyebrow. "And once you get there? You said Nox wrote about hostile natives, not to mention you have no idea how to read anything that might be written there."

"Maybe the locals can be reasoned with if you aren't a manipulative asshole, looking to gain more dark power for your own use. Or maybe they were just a tribe that lived nearby that we might be able to avoid."

"We?" Matalina asked, looking up from the pages in her hand.

Dean winced. "There's a catch to all of this. Even knowing where the place was, Nox wrote that it was impossible to find without the spirit's help. He had to...enlist the help of a spirit of that particular jungle in order to find it."

"Meaning you need a shaman to do it. One that we don't have," Samuel said flatly.

And none that they could ask to help them, especially considering the last one to help the pack had been kidnapped while under their protection. "We have something close."

"You intend to drag Silun into this? He's just a boy," Mikael asked, his words pointed and bordering on accusatory.

"First of all, I'm not going to *drag* him into anything. My plan was to explain it to him and see if he was willing to go. It would be his decision, and an informed decision at that. Secondly, he's more adult than anyone his age has any right to be. Being stuck in Damian's hands for a couple of months will do that to a person."

"That's part of my point, Dean. He's been through enough, don't you think?"

Dean turned to Samuel. "I've wondered before, so I'm going to ask now, what's the age of adulthood with werewolves?"

Samuel's gaze was locked on his son, "Sixteen."

"And I believe Silun turned seventeen a month ago, didn't he?" Dean asked again.

"Yes."

"Dean," Mikael protested, sounding as if he were fighting to keep the frustration out of his voice now that Samuel was paying attention to him.

"I'm not saying we throw him into some battle or make him take point. But if I know him like I think I do, he would want to at least be asked. I'm not going to sit around and pretend he can't help if he wants to. He deserves the chance to decide for himself, not to be treated like he's made of glass."

The not so subtle reminder of their earlier argument earned him a dirty look and silence from Mikael. That was at least familiar to Dean. The silence had been sitting between them ever since their argument after Eveline's arrival in the Grove. The only words they had spoken to one another had been cool exchanges of perfunctory conversation. If they didn't have to speak to one another, they didn't.

"Do you have an issue with this crusade of his?" Samuel asked Mikael.

Dean froze at that. He hadn't expected Samuel to outright ask if Mikael was onboard. He had never included Mikael directly in any decision before, not when it came to one of Dean's ideas. Then again, Mikael had always explicitly supported Dean before now. It was obvious that Mikael was taking issue with it this time and wasn't bothering to hide it. Dean didn't miss the fact that Samuel had also referred to this as one of his 'crusades'. Like father, like son apparently.

After a long silence, Mikael shrugged. "He's never been wrong before, has he? If he says this is a good place to start, then I agree with him. If he says that knowing more about the crystals will help find them, then it's probably true."

"But?"

Mikael shook his head. "No buts, that's it."

As Samuel's eyes searched Mikael's face, Dean felt relief permeate through him. It would have been so easy for Mikael to throw a wrench in his idea. Samuel had been a little too eager to hear Mikael's opinion on the matter. If Dean were feeling cynical, he would say it was because Samuel was hoping for a good reason to shoot Dean's idea down. That Mikael hadn't done so left the alpha without an easy out.

Mikael glanced away from Samuel to Dean, as if sensing his thoughts. When Dean returned the glance, Mikael's face stiffened before facing forward once more. Mikael might not have thrown Dean's idea under the bus, but their argument wasn't over. Dean loved Mikael all the more for still standing by him and not bringing his father into their argument. That didn't change the fact that Dean hated how Mikael was suddenly trying to treat him with kid gloves. He loved Mikael fiercely, but dammit he was still mad at him.

"Right," Samuel grunted, sounding mildly disappointed. He glanced to his mate, who smiled a little and shrugged. Dean couldn't tell if that smile was about him and Mikael, or if it was because Samuel was put out. The woman could be as mischievous as she was perceptive, and he knew any of them could be the source of her amusement.

"Is that a yes?" Dean asked, growing impatient at the pause in proceedings.

Samuel sighed. "If I'm honest, I want to say no. We may not be at war, but having our pack at full strength seems a wise decision to me. Yet I'm also not willing to deny your track record, especially after I supported one of your plans that came from a just a dream. You have something more concrete to work off this time, something to actually backup your instincts. And you can quit looking smug about it, too."

Dean straightened his face quickly. "Wasn't trying to, I promise."

Samuel's mouth twisted in disapproval as he continued. "I also see no point in changing what worked before. Dante and Apollo will go with you. Dante is one of the best trackers we have, and he'll learn the land quicker than anyone else I could send. Apollo might know a lot about the human world, but he's still a scout, and as silent as they come. I imagine that will come in handy. Both of them are skilled fighters, but Katarina is still your best bet in a fight."

Dean grinned. "That and I'm sure she's getting restless again, since you've been keeping everyone close to home."

Samuel barely repressed a sigh. "Yes, there is that. And we've already established that where you go, my son goes, too. Now, this all hinges on whether Silun agrees. I cannot and will not order him to go, as he's not part of this pack. You wish him to make his own decision, so I leave discussing it with him in your hands. If he doesn't wish to go, it will be on you to convince one of the other packs with a shaman to volunteer to help."

Dean didn't know if that was Samuel's way of giving Dean more responsibility or just a way for him not to support it further. Dean knew it didn't matter if Samuel helped further or not. With everything that had happened, the chances of another pack willingly volunteering their shaman for something like this was extremely low. If Silun didn't agree to it, there wouldn't be much chance of it happening at all.

CHAPTER 8

"You really think that trekking into the middle of the jungle is a good idea?"

Dean looked up from the table strewn with papers. After asking Silun to come visit him, when he got a chance, Dean had busied himself pouring over everything he had. Even with plenty of skilled people coming, he wanted to be absolutely sure his findings were accurate. He had been confident enough that he was right to bring it before Samuel, but he had to have a better plan in mind than the one he'd had when they set off to find the shamans.

"Everything here points to that being the best place to look. Like I told everyone else, those crystals have to go and this is the best place to start to find out how."

Silun shuddered. "I don't want to think of what it would be like if someone else was using even one of those crystals. Wouldn't it require shamans of power, though?"

"Do you think that's the only way to power up the crystals?" Dean asked, genuinely interested to know Silun's thoughts on the matter.

Silun chewed his bottom lip as he shook his head. "No. I

don't have any real reason to think it, but anything that evil probably has more than one way to work. Nothing is ever easy for the good guys."

Dean thought about that for a moment, turning in his chair to face Silun. "When you were around the crystal Damian had, what did you feel from it?"

"Feel? It felt like death, darkness. It was like...I don't know, like something was eating at me from the inside. I wanted to run away from it, but it was as though being near it made me so cold I couldn't move. Freakiest thing."

Dean mulled that over, finding that it about matched his own memory. It was the same feeling he had when he'd sensed the dark power within Nox, or close to it anyway. If he were honest, there had been something different about the crystal's power. It had felt darker and even more twisted when it had come from Nox. He didn't know if it was his own perception or Nox altering his memory, but he would swear it was somehow worse coming from Nox. It was no less terrifying when the power came directly from the crystal, but he remembered it feeling almost less...corrupted.

"You're doing that zoning out thing again."

"Oh, sorry," Dean apologized, smiling a little sheepishly.

"It's all good, it wasn't the bad kind. You just looked like you were on a whole different planet."

Dean chuckled. "I do that when I'm thinking hard about something that's caught my interest. I even did it as a kid."

Silun shrugged. "I talked a lot. Couldn't get me to shut up."

Dean remembered Dante griping about Silun being overly chatty. "Somehow I think that hasn't really changed much."

Silun stuck his tongue out, looking more his age than he normally did. "Yeah, yeah. But hey, how are you planning on getting out there?"

"Apollo apparently knows a way to get plane tickets really cheap. He made it sound super cheap, cheaper than you should be able to. Don't know how he managed that, because he only smirked at me when I asked. Apollo isn't really the smirking type, so that was a little weird."

Silun laughed. "It's kinda cool to see that he's got a sense of humor. But if it makes you feel better, a lot of packs nowadays have someone who's good for that sort of thing. Kinda think they trade secrets or something too, because they're all pretty good at it. Probably means he's got the whole passport thing taken care of, too."

Dean straightened at that, glancing down at the spread of notes he had been making. "Oh hell. I completely forgot about passports, including my own."

"Apollo seems like the kind of guy to ask if he thought he needed to. Probably taking care of yours for you. Don't know if that makes him really helpful, or if it's just part of that sneaky thing he does."

"Bit of both, I think."

"You and Mikael still not talking to each other?"

Dean squinted at Silun. "What do you mean?"

Silun rolled his eyes. "You guys haven't made deliberate eye contact since you got those pages from Damian's journal. I mean it's pretty obvious you guys aren't getting along right now."

"We're fine," Dean replied, looking back to the table.

"Not what I asked. I didn't think you guys were gonna break up or...whatever mates do when they stop being together. I might not have been in a relationship before, but even I know people fight."

"All wise in the ways of the world?" Dean asked sarcastically.

"Wow, cranky much? Sorry I asked."

He sighed, immediately regretting his attitude. "Sorry. No, you're right. We're not talking very much right now. He's not happy with me because I'm trying to do this and I'm not happy because he keeps treating me like I might break at any minute. You know, like you insinuated, even my damn neighbors acted like that."

"Hey, hold on a second. I didn't mean to give you that impression, dude. It's not like I think you're going to crack or something. And I'm betting Mikael doesn't think that either. We're just worried about you, Dean. A lot of stuff has happened to you, but it doesn't make you weak or whatever. Just means you're a person who's been through some rough stuff."

"It's not like you were having a picnic," Dean pointed out, his annoyance returning.

"Yeah, thanks for reminding me. But you know what? I've been talking about it, trying to get past it. You've just been ignoring it and hoping it will go away."

Dean wanted to argue with him, but even as irritated as he was, he couldn't bring himself to do much more than glare at Silun. From what he knew, Silun really had been trying to get over everything that happened to him, confiding in Dante of all people. That, and Dean actually hadn't been doing anything of the sort. Silun had hit the nail on the head about Dean trying to avoid it until it went away, but Dean's pride refused to allow him to admit it.

"Anyway, my relationship or mental health isn't why I asked you to come visit."

Silun looked like he was about to argue before clicking

his tongue. "Okay, then why did you ask me to come visit you?"

Dean took a deep breath, shifting the page about a spirit guide into view. "Our little group isn't complete."

"What? You need more than the best tracker, scout, and fighter you guys have?"

Dean fidgeted with the page, struck by nerves all of a sudden as he went on to explain. "Damian's notes...on Nox's notes, describe how Nox needed a guide to get to the temple. A spirit guide."

Silun leaned back, eyes tracking all over the room as he spoke. "That's right. Nox was a shaman, wasn't he?"

"Yeah, he was. Apparently they could only get so far into the jungle without help. Nox found himself a spirit and used it as a guide. I'm betting any shaman could do it and without having to bully them like I'm sure he did."

Silun shook his head. "I know what you're asking, but I'm not a shaman, Dean."

"You're not officially a full-fledged shaman, but you can talk to spirits. That's all that's needed for this to work."

Silun looked down at his lap. "I don't know, Dean."

"That's why I'm asking you, instead of telling. I'm not going to try to make or convince you to do this. I might not have said it yet, but I'm not going to sit around and pretend there's no danger in this trip. We're going out into the middle of nowhere, in an environment none of us really know anything about. We're looking for some hidden temple that Nox described as having angry natives nearby. There's a huge chance of something going wrong and for something really bad to happen."

Silun looked up, a small smile on his face. "You really know how to sell it, you know that?"

"I'm not trying to sell it. I'm telling you the truth. I think you're able to make your own decision on this. Which is kind of why I waited till after I pretty much told you everything before I brought it up. I didn't want you to be weighing everything up in your mind instead of taking everything in."

"Know me that well, already?"

Dean shrugged. "You take a lot of stuff onto your shoulders really easily. I didn't want you to listen to every piece of info and think that each one was an argument for why you should or shouldn't go. You've already made your mind up on what you think about what we're doing, otherwise you would have argued with me. Now I'm asking if you want to be a part of it."

"No pressure or anything."

"I'm not going to say there isn't, because it's going to feel like a big decision no matter what I say now. But, it's not going to matter what you say Silun. I'll respect your decision and none of us are going to think badly of you if you don't want to do this. You've had enough danger in your life. It's not a bad thing if you don't want to throw yourself into another situation so easily."

"None of you, huh?"

Dean eyed him suspiciously. "And don't go making this decision based on what you think Dante might think or say either."

"If I do that, I have to go and take responsibility for whatever I choose."

That made Dean smile. "Welcome to being all grown up."

Silun picked up a pillow from the couch and threw it at Dean. "Anyone ever told you you're a brat?"

Dean caught it with a laugh. "More than you think, or maybe not."

"I'm scared. Not of what could happen, but of what I might do."

The abrupt change of tone to one of guilt had Dean leaving his chair to move closer to Silun. "What's that supposed to mean?"

Silun looked hopelessly at him. "Oh, come on Dean. When we were in that room, I didn't do anything when you and Apollo were under attack. I just hid and tried to get the shamans unstrapped. Couldn't even do that right."

"That's exactly where I wanted you to be, out of the fray."

Silun huffed "So what? It's okay for you to be in the thick of things, but not me?"

Dean shook his head. "You had spent months locked in a dark cell. If you tried to help, you would have just gotten hurt. But you're forgetting the part where you forgot all about being weak and tired. You know, the part where you kept up with us as we escaped. Even helping me with Apollo when he was hurt. Then there was the part where you shouted down a certain grumpy werewolf that you're crushing on."

Silun blushed at the reminder. "Was kind of hoping you wouldn't remember that."

"What? Watching you yell at Dante so he would behave? Never."

"He still hasn't let me live that down, you know."

Dean snorted. "Let's remember that my first interaction with him resulted in him being scarred for life. I think if he can get over that with good grace, he can get over the fact that you raised your voice at him. Honestly? I don't think he really respects someone unless they stand up to him."

"That...sounds like him."

"But that's my point Silun. You're not weak or a coward.

You can't beat yourself up just because you stayed out of harm's way when everything hit the fan. You're tougher than you give yourself credit for."

Silun gave Dean a little smirk. "You sound like Dante now."

"He give you the same speech?"

"Yeah, just with more swearing. And a lot of hand gestures."

Dean reached out and squeezed Silun's arm with a snicker. "Sounds like him."

Silun patted Dean's hand, nodding. "It does. But I'll make you a deal."

"A deal?"

"If I promise to try and stop coming down too hard on myself, you'll try to stop pretending like you're not hurting. You know, actually talk to someone. I'd suggest Mikael, but anyone will do."

Dean frowned, not liking the sudden boxed-in feeling that Silun's proposal gave him. If he refused, he would essentially be telling Silun not to help himself. If he agreed and didn't at least make an attempt, he would be a hypocrite. There was no way around Silun's deal without both agreeing to and actually making a genuine attempt to follow through. Silun had him nicely pinned and the impish gleam in his eyes told Dean he knew it, too.

"You're a little cheater, you know that right?"

"Yes sir."

Dean grunted, his only show of annoyance. "Fine, deal."

"Sweet!" Silun proclaimed as he stood up and walked to the front door. "So, when are we leaving?"

Dean twisted to look over the back of the couch at Silun, surprise written all over his face. "Wait, you want to go?"

Silun shrugged. "Consider it me trying to do something outside my comfort zone. To prove that I'm not some wimp."

"Uh, that wasn't really what I meant when I said all that."

"Okay, but it's true. How about I owe you guys something besides what I've done here? Or maybe I'm worried about what kind of medical treatment you guys might get if one of you is hurt and I'm not there. I've seen what kind of first aid you guys do and it's not pretty. The idea that I'd like to keep an eye on Dante, even if it is because of a stupid crush? All of those are genuine answers I could give, and they'd all be right. Does it matter why I do it, if I believe that it's the right thing to do?"

Before Dean could respond, Silun walked out with a little wave. It seemed oddly quiet in the moments after he left. The shaman in training had left him to think long and hard. Not about the next big adventure that Dean had laid out for them, or how to prepare for it. Instead, he sat on the couch, wondering how someone Silun's age seemed to have more sense and wisdom than he did.

CHAPTER 9

Dean didn't want to say it out loud. That he thought it was hilarious Mikael was apparently prone to air sickness, but he was certainly thinking it. It had come as a surprise to Dean on the first flight. Now that they were on their third one, Dean was fighting to hide his smile. It was mostly due to the dramatic way Mikael was acting. When he wasn't trying not to throw up, he was muttering under his breath, mostly a string of words Dean didn't hear him use very often.

"Stupid human travel," he groused for what Dean believed was close to the hundredth time.

"It was the quickest way we had and the cheapest. Have you seen gas prices lately?" Dean told Mikael, still fighting to hide his smile.

"No Dean, I didn't notice, what with the big ass truck I drive."

Dean reached over and patted Mikael's knee in what he hoped was a consoling gesture. Somewhere between their flights, they had set their argument aside in favor of Dean attempting to comfort Mikael. He knew they weren't over the argument yet; but it was on standby for now. Mikael was a bit too preoccupied with his upset stomach to really hold onto his anger. Privately, Dean was just happy to have a conversation that wasn't either short or somewhat curt.

"Is it stubbornness that's kept you from throwing up or just a really strong stomach?"

Mikael squinted at him. "You're enjoying this."

Dean shook his head, even as he continued to still fight off a smile. "It's more like, I never get to see you like this."

"Sick?"

"I was going to say cranky and complaining. I think I'm getting a good idea of what you would be like as a patient, if you ever do catch something. Wait, do you guys actually get sick?"

"Obviously."

Dean poked Mikael's thigh. "You know what I mean."

Mikael shuddered as he rubbed his stomach. "We can, yeah. Doesn't happen all that much, but yeah."

"No wonder you're a little...uh, off about being a bit airsick."

"A bit?"

"You haven't actually puked yet, so I would say a bit, yeah. But I guess that's just me."

"You wait until you get sick and watch me remind you of this moment."

"I'm actually really surprised you haven't had to deal with it yet. I usually get sick at least once a year, maybe it's the whole druid thing."

Mikael shrugged, looking like he was afraid to open his mouth as the cabin rocked once more. It wouldn't have been from fear of being overheard. Save for their group, there wasn't one person on the small plane that spoke the slightest bit of English. The advantage to that was they could speak freely without fear of saying the wrong thing. The disadvantage was that communicating with people was a slow and painful process that involved checking the phone for translations.

"Should have just bought a fancy app or something," he mumbled to himself.

Mikael's silent struggle with airsickness continued for the remainder of the flight. Dean was genuinely pleased to see that Mikael had managed to keep his stomach contents down. He wasn't about to tell him, though, and risk getting another dirty look. Mikael didn't make it easy on Dean when he all but ran out of the plane, looking as if he wanted to kiss the ground in relief.

"Can we please run or drive on the way back?" Mikael asked, the color in his face returning now that they were on solid ground.

"I'm not running back home Mikael," Dean told him as he glanced around to see where the others had wandered off to. They had been closer to the door of the plane, and it wasn't like the building they were in was all that large. The whole plot could only be called an airport because it had a runway and a building for people to exit out into.

"They go outside already?" Mikael asked.

"I don't see them, so let's go find out. Maybe one of them has figured out a way to get us transportation."

That ended up being the one detail Dean hadn't been able to figure out himself. If they had been dealing with a major airport, it would have been a different story. They were about as far out in the middle of nowhere as they could reach by plane, so a rental was out of the question. Dean had brought some of his savings from the previous season, having already exchanged it by the time they reached the final landing strip. That was in case they could manage to find someone willing to sell their vehicle, but he wasn't too sure how that would pan out.

They stepped into the sticky heat outside the building, spotting the rest of their group standing in what looked like it served as the airport parking lot. A glance at them had him immediately concerned that someone might want to just take a vehicle instead of buying one. He didn't know if any of them knew how to hotwire one, but he didn't doubt that they would if they had to. His little trip with Apollo showed just how willing they were to bend or break the law. Then again, Dean had been on board with that as well, so he probably didn't have much room to judge.

"I didn't know it was possible for it to be this hot outside without there being a large fire somewhere around," Katarina grumped as they approached. From the looks of it, she was tolerating the weather about as well as Mikael had tolerated the trip on the plane. Dante seemed to be faring better, but him and Apollo were used to toughing out the elements. Silun appeared to be about where Dean was, as miserable as Katarina, but attempting to hide it.

"Welcome to jungle weather," Dean told her brightly, unwilling to pass up the chance to tease her. It earned him the glare he expected, but that was about it. Katarina probably wouldn't move more than was absolutely necessary. Not only was it hot, but the air was thick enough that he would swear you could see it.

Dean glanced around, noticing someone was missing. "And where's Apollo?"

"Probably off trying to find us a ride. Here's hoping he just steals a van with some AC in it," Dante grumbled.

"Oh God, yes please. This is the worst," Katarina said.

Dean glanced at Mikael, who was watching in quiet amusement. "You guys do know it's probably going to be worse out in the middle of the jungle, right? And we can't just take the AC with us after we set out on foot."

"Yeah, but this way, I can say I know what air conditioning felt like after being in this heat. That'll make up for it," Katarina said.

Dean raised a brow slowly. "I don't think that's how that works, but sure."

"Makes sense to me, that's all that matters," Katarina bit back, irritation simmering beneath her attempt at being jovial.

Dean wanted to make a teasing comment about "female logic" but decided against it after a quick glance at her face. She was doing a good job of keeping her mood in check, better than the men of the group usually did anyway. He didn't relish the idea of poking the bear, or werewolf, and risk having her snap at him. They had a long and rough journey ahead of them and he didn't want to start off by having Katarina and him getting into it over a silly joke.

Within a half hour, a large, beat-up van rumbled up beside where they stood, still in abject discomfort. Apollo sat behind the wheel, looking about as pleased with himself as the stoic man could without giving anything away. Dean stepped up to the driver's side window as Apollo rolled it down, and sighed as the welcome feel of cool air rushed out of the cab to brush across his face.

"Well, you'll have made Kat's day," Dean told him, grinning.

"It's what I live for," Apollo replied quietly.

"Thought it was to make me happy and worship the ground I walked on," Dante teased as he opened the side door and disappeared from Dean's view.

Apollo rolled his eyes, rolling up his window in response rather than saying anything. He wasn't fooling

Dean however, who saw the corner of Apollo's mouth twitch as he fought a smile. Only people who had seen the man beneath the expressionless mask were comfortable enough to tease Apollo. They were also the only people who got any sort of reaction out of him that he didn't first give himself permission to show. Of course, Dean didn't think he had ever seen anyone get Apollo to watch them with the same shadow of a smile as he was giving Dante right now.

"Ya getting in?" Kat asked from somewhere in the shadows of the van's interior.

Mikael leaned forward so he was in Dean's sight, a knowing smirk on his face, "When he comes back from whatever thoughts he's lost himself in."

Dean turned and swatted Mikael's broad chest playfully. "I was thinking ahead was all."

The look on his mate's face told Dean he didn't believe a word of it, but Mikael said nothing. There was only a lingering, knowing look before he crawled into the van, amidst protests of "long legs" and him being "all elbows." Dean couldn't help but glance at Apollo one more time, the scout looking back at him with a wry expression. He didn't say it, but he was pretty sure Apollo was thinking along the same lines as he was. What had started off as a mission to possibly help the world was quickly turning into a family road trip, complete with the squabbling and teasing that came with it.

Filing that little curiosity away for later, he peered into the open door of the van, seeing no room for him, "What, am I gonna be sitting on someone's lap now?"

Kat popped her head out from the far back row of seats, "I'm betting you're on his lap enough times anyway. You're up front, Mom."

"Mom?" Dean asked, trying to sound huffy but coming off like he was trying not to laugh instead.

"Apollo's too quiet to be Mom, plus he's driving. Doesn't Dad always do the driving?"

Apparently he wasn't the only one who had the family road trip comparison spring to mind. It was also dawning on him that she wasn't kidding about him being up front. Just as with their rescue mission into the mountains, the group was leaving leadership of this particular trip up to Dean. She might have phrased it like she was teasing him, but she was really just telling him he was still the boss man.

He shot a worried glance toward Mikael, but shrugged at the rest of them as he made his way around the van. It didn't surprise him, since this had been his idea and he was the one who had the most information to work with, little as that was. The last mission he had been in charge of had disintegrated rapidly within no time, after entering the mountains. Yes, they had ended the war, killed Damian, and they'd all left with their lives and limbs intact. It still felt like a disaster to him, or at least something he wouldn't want to throw on his resume. Yet here he was, in charge again, with the others looking to him for guidance, when he barely knew a damn thing himself.

"Where to?" Apollo asked quietly from beside him as he made himself comfortable in the cool air of the van.

Dean shrugged, pulling out the map he'd cobbled together and starting to comb over it. No one said anything to him as he began to trace the route they were going to be taking, or hopefully taking. He had felt so confident about this trip while he had been safely back in the Grove and now doubt filled him. The maps, once deemed the closest he was going to get to accuracy, looked like the haphazard work of a child. They were working with so very little information, based on human who barely knew his head from his ass when it came to this sort of knowledge.

Why the hell had they put him in charge again?

"Dean?"

Mikael's voice was soft behind him. Immediately, Dean felt the tension that had been building in his shoulders ease. His mate's strong hand wrapped around his elbow and held there. He said nothing else, and the others chatted away restlessly in the back, oblivious to what passed between the two of them. Only Apollo seemed to be privy to this private moment, but he was doing a fine job of pretending to pay attention to something else.

Smiling, more to himself than anyone else, since Mikael couldn't see his face, he reached back to stroke Mikael's long fingers. He was grateful for Mikael's almost instant insight into the contents of his heart. Whether it was due to their bond through the mating, or simply through Mikael knowing Dean that well, it didn't matter. What mattered was that Mikael knew his feelings, but more importantly, he knew the best and most direct way to address them. His name, and a light touch, that was all it took to quell the storm of panic that had been threatening to build within him.

He took a deep breath, "The best we're going to do is to get to a place a few hours north of here. It's not going to be a precise location, but so long as we're decently close, it will work."

"Flying by the seat of our pants, then?" Silun asked from his seat.

Now there was a phrase Dean hadn't heard since he was a kid, and it made him smile. "That's about the gist of it, yeah."

"Well, your last plan like that worked out pretty good

for me, so let's get to it," Dean could hear the smile in Silun's voice.

Dean glanced at Apollo, who was now looking back expectantly. He jammed his thumb in the direction that they would have to take. Apollo hummed softly, glancing in the rearview mirror one more time before gunning the engine and pulling out of the lot.

CHAPTER 10

"Well, this looks...inviting," Kat quipped as they stood on the opposite side of the road from where they had hidden the van.

Then again, calling the path they were on a *road* might be a bit much. Saying that they had hidden the van could be an exaggeration as well. Dean was pretty sure the road leading into the Grove was better cared for than the narrow, hole-strewn path Apollo had driven them down. It also wasn't so much hiding the van as it had been driving it into the safest patch of jungle Apollo could find.

The only thing stopping them from walking into the jungle right now was the moment of anticipation. After only an hour of driving, the jungle had begun to close in on either side of the road. As it grew thicker and wilder, so too had the road grown worse, more dilapidated and rundown. By the time they reached where Dean estimated where they would need to stop, the jungle had blossomed into an intimidating wall of unknown greenery around them.

Now they were only waiting for Dean to give the go ahead, as they paced restlessly along the edge of the jungle.

They were anxious to get started, but not so pushy that they weren't willing to allow Dean a few moments to get his bearings. It was a strange world, totally different to the forests and fields they were familiar with. Everyone knew just how dangerous the jungle could be, especially when they didn't have much to help them avoid the dangers except their wits and what little information Dean had been able to dig up before they left.

For his part, Dean hadn't felt the same wariness. He had already committed fully to this, and had rid himself of his overwhelming worry back at the airstrip. Now there was only the thrill of the unknown and that had always excited him, albeit privately at times. It was a strange world for him too, but that was something he could handle. Ever since he had left the predictability of his safe world behind him to move back to his grandfather's property, he had been thrown into many different levels of the strange and unknown.

This was just one more level, and he was going to meet it like he had all the others.

"Smells weird," Dante commented, this time aiming his words in Dean's direction.

Knowing it was a ploy to get his attention, Dean looked up with a smile. "I can't imagine it'll smell anymore familiar when we get further in. What's it smell like to you guys?"

The werewolves all looked at one another and shrugged, almost as one. Dean laughed at them, amused by the bewildered expressions on their faces. It was the same look he got from Mikael whenever his mate tried to explain his well-honed senses. Either werewolf senses worked on such a level that human language couldn't properly describe them or he was traveling with a bunch of werewolves who just lacked the ability to put it into words. Either way, the mirrored looks of bewilderment definitely made them look like a family.

"Well, you guys are really helpful," he commented, folding up the map and stuffing it into the side pocket of his bag.

"So, what's the plan?" Kat asked, allowing her impatience to shine through.

"We head east until we find the river that's supposed to be in that direction. You guys are going to have to be the lead on that, since you can smell a water source better than I can," Dean explained as he checked the compass strapped to his wrist.

"You think we can just smell water?" Kat asked.

"Kat," Mikael groaned. "Please don't."

"Alright, well, if everyone is done complaining? We kind of have to get moving if we want to make progress. Dunno about you guys, but I would rather get a feel for everything while we have daylight so we can figure out what good places to make camp look like, rather than stumbling around in the dark and hoping for the best."

They all peered at him now, at least two sets of eyebrows raising as he finished speaking. "What?"

"You're...perky," Dante commented, somehow making the description sound like an insult.

"Motivated. Now let's get going," Dean grunted, scowling at them to cover up the energy bubbling up inside of him.

Sighing, and with a roll of his eyes, Apollo took the first steps into the jungle. It was a testament to how thick the foliage was when the scout disappeared from sight almost immediately. Dante grunted his annoyance and followed after him, mumbling about how he should have been the one taking point. Nobody, least of all Apollo, paid Dante any mind when he got to grumbling, but it still made Dean smile every now and then.

With two of their party already making their way into the jungle, the rest of them followed. Dean found himself in the middle of the group as they began to move forward with Silun right behind him. Dean realized they were the center of their little group. He and Silun were probably the most important elements in finding what they were looking for, but they were also the most vulnerable members of the party. Silun might be a werewolf, but he suffered from the same flaw that Dean did: a lack of real combat training and very little experience in battle. Neither of them took issue with the unconscious formation that the others had taken, pride taking a backseat to practicality.

Back home, Dean would have expected the flora to steadily grow wilder the further they walked away from the road. The jungle didn't adhere to that expectation. The moment they pushed through the first line of plants, it had exploded out before them. There was no denying the vitality the jungle possessed as they pushed through thick branches and stepped around heavy bushes. Everything here was so colorful, even the expected variety of green hues seemed more vivid and vibrant.

Dean could see what Dante meant about the smell as they progressed deeper. There was something strange about the way the jungle smelled. The flowering plants were definitely more pungent than the ones near their home. It was more than that, though. There was something beneath all of it that he couldn't quite describe. He didn't know if there was a word for it or if he would have better luck describing it if he could smell it as the others could.

They walked for a couple of hours, mostly quiet as they tried to adjust to the strange environment. There was always something new to see: a plant or something moving in the trees above their heads or on the jungle floor below their feet. For every new and interesting plant or animal they saw, there always seemed to be something that seemed equally dangerous. The curious noise of a pack of strange monkeys would give way to a hiss from one of them as they spotted what could have been a snake through the thick foliage that covered the jungle floor. The werewolves of the group would probably cope better with the bite of a venomous snake, but it didn't mean any of them wanted to risk it. There were many unknown dangers in this place, and they were all tense and wary.

Except Dean, who was more enraptured by what he saw than nervous. He didn't know if it was because he was better equipped to being thrown into a strange environment or if it was something else. The same could be said of Silun, who seemed to share Dean's amazement and lack of fear. Dean thought it was interesting and a bit of a conundrum that the two most vulnerable members of the group were also the ones who were the least afraid.

"So, does it feel different to ya?" Kat's voice came from behind him, having pushed ahead of Mikael and Silun to walk beside Dean.

"Feel different?" Dean asked.

"Yeah, ya asked if the place smelled different to us because of our noses. Well, you're the one who gets all touchy feely with the forest and plants, this place feel any different to you?"

Dean eyed her, smiling a little. "Really?"

"What?"

"You never ask me that sort of thing. Just seems kind of funny coming from you, I guess."

She jammed her thumb over her shoulder with a grunt.

"Well, my brother ain't that great company. He's tense and worrying about your safety, so he's boring. Silun is off in his own little world and I don't wanna distract Dante or Apollo. It's hot, I'm tired of thinking about how hot it is, and I wanna be distracted."

"Okay, but I haven't really thought about it."

Katarina seemed surprised at that. "Really? I would have thought that woulda been the first thing you did when you got close enough. You've been vibrating out of your skin since we got in here. Figured it was because you were onto something."

Unconsciously, Dean glanced down at himself. "I haven't been vibrating out of my skin!"

"Uh huh. So, why don't you take a peek?"

Dean huffed, wanting to argue the point further, but deciding against it. Just as before, he no sooner wanted to have a testy Katarina pissed off at him than he wanted to anger a bear. It wasn't so much the thought that she would actually do anything to him, but he didn't want to deal with her being angry, either. The woman might be an excellent warrior, but he was pretty sure that her wrath could extend beyond the physical if she wanted it to.

He waited until the next time Apollo and Dante paused to see if they could sense water, before he tried to reach out with his mind. His eyes closed and his mind expanded with an ease he would have struggled with only months before. His practice with his powers was beginning to pay off and a sense of peace washed over him as his senses expanded beyond the normal scope, out into the wild environment around him.

The sensation rushed in with such potency it almost overwhelmed him. He hissed, a sharp intake of breath, staggering slightly as he pulled his mind back, away from the jungle surrounding him. Dimly, he could sense Katarina's iron grip on his arms, helping to hold him up as he heard Mikael demand to know what was wrong. Dean couldn't tell if he was going to pass out or if he was riding some sort of high.

"Dean?" Mikael's voice, closer this time, more urgent.

"I'm okay. Holy hell, I'm okay," Dean assured him, his own voice sounding more distant than it should have.

He wasn't sure if that was the truth, but it was the best he could come up with as he tried to get his head to work, while Mikael panicked next to him. If he thought the jungle had seemed alive before, it was nothing compared to when he had expanded his senses outward. The entire area around them had exploded with the pure sensation of life the moment he had tried to reach outward toward it. He struggled to pull his senses back right from the moment he had released them but the pull of the energies around him was so great he could barely keep himself in one place.

It was definitely due to the sheer amount of life around him, that much he knew. Everything here was so full of vibrancy that it felt as if the jungle was burning with it. It was almost painful to touch. It was so overwhelming that the closest description he could use to explain the sensation was pain. If it had been a noise, it would have deafened him, and if it was light, it would have blinded him. He was in awe, and more than a little worried for himself, as he struggled to pull the last bits of his mind back away from the world around him.

"Hell, this is not the woods at home," he muttered, more to himself than the others.

"What did you see?" Mikael asked, his grip having replaced Katarina's at some point while Dean had been struggling to get his mind to cooperate.

"See? I didn't see much, but geez did I feel it. This place is...alive. Everything back home is living, but it's...calmer? I don't know how to describe it since I only felt it for a moment. This jungle is so full of life that I can't sense anything without it drowning me. I don't know if there's even any sort of mind to this jungle like there is to the forest or there was to the mountain."

"You...drowned in it?" Mikael asked slowly, sounding worried but trying to hide it.

Dean shook his head slowly, trying to clear it, "No, but it felt like I could have. It was like...turning on the radio in the car and forgetting you had it on a rock station the night before, at almost full blast. It was all just there, in my face, or my...whatever it is that I have when I'm doing my thing. There's no real order here, no real...I don't know. It's chaos. If this place does have a mind, it's either insane, or would seem that way to us, enough that it wouldn't make a difference either way."

He could tell they didn't understand. Everyone but Silun seemed to be confused by his explanation. The shaman in training was looking at him with a curious expression. Dean couldn't tell if the younger man had tried to expand his own unique sense out yet and had a different experience. The look on his face gave nothing away, only a thoughtful wonder as his gaze slipped away to stare deeper into the forest.

"Guess that explains why you've been bouncing off the walls, er, trees," Kat corrected herself, shrugging away her own confusion.

Dean wasn't really sure he'd been all that energetic, but he couldn't argue with her reasoning either. If being around a huge variety of living things, such as the forest, calmed him, why not the presence of something else? The mountain had affected him, even granted him a few things at the right moment. It was possible that just existing in the jungle was enough for some of its frantic energy to have leached its way into him. The problem with all of those things was that he had no control over what did or didn't affect him. If she was right and the jungle really was altering his energy or personality, he didn't know how he would try and catch it, or be able to try and stop it.

"You okay to continue?" Dante asked, looking eager to keep moving.

"Yeah," Dean replied.

He shook his head at Mikael's questioning look, not wanting to get into a long discussion over it right now. Dean needed time to process all that had happened in such a short time. None of them were familiar with this land, nor with Dean's abilities. Those were two unknowns in play and Dean couldn't say he was too surprised to find out it wasn't a very smooth meeting. He really wished he had the ability to try and sense the jungle with a bit more caution. Maybe there was something to what Kat said, because he felt he would normally have been more wary about shoving his vulnerable mind out into the world like that.

"Okay, because I'm pretty sure we're getting close to that river of yours," Dante continued, now looking at Mikael. Dean couldn't see Mikael's face, now that he was turned away from Dean to look at Dante. He was aware that there was some sort of silent communication going on between the cousin's, but Dean didn't care. They couldn't stand around and wait for Dean to be perfectly alright to continue. That would take too long, especially if the headache he could feel coming on was any indication.

Within what seemed like a half hour, Dante was proven right in his assessment of where they were. The sound of the river was buried beneath the sounds of the jungle, but it was there when they got close enough. It wasn't the strongest current he had ever seen, but it was still strong enough that it would be a chore to cross.

"This your river?" Dante asked as he glanced up and down its flow.

Dean patted the pocket where the map lay. "It's the only river around here that we know about. We need to get to the other side and then head north."

"For how long?" Mikael asked, squinting up river as if assessing it.

"Until we reach elevated ground."

Mikael glanced at him. "How elevated?"

"Elevated enough to be noticeable. Big hills, most likely. It was hard to tell, I didn't exactly get a topographical map to study the place, even if one existed to begin with."

Apollo nodded, speaking slowly. "It's getting late. We'll cross the river now and try to find a place to camp on the other side. I don't know the exact best spots to make camp, but by a river should do us well for now."

Silun glanced at the other side of the river nervously. "Correct me if I'm wrong, but isn't a river where animals, including you know, big predators, go to drink?"

Dante laughed. "What, afraid of cats?"

"Cats that live around here? Definitely," Silun answered without shame.

"Most wild animals aren't too keen on any light that isn't natural. We'll keep a fire going throughout the night and have someone on watch, someone with good ears and eyes." Apollo replied.

That meant Dean wasn't going to be chosen for sentry duty during the night. It should have bothered him that he wasn't going to be put to work, but he understood the logic behind it. He might have been able to offer himself up if he could have spoken with the jungle. Dean was definitely going to try to make contact with it again, but a little more carefully this time. He didn't want to push having him on watch without knowing if his attempts to make sense of the thriving chaos around them would be effective.

"Well, if that's our best option, let's get to it already," Katarina added, making her way to the river's edge.

CHAPTER 11

Making a fire had proven to be a more difficult task in practice than it had sounded in theory. With everything so alive and damp, they had struggled to find even enough kindling to get the fire going. The fact that they didn't dare go too far away from camp, and thus one another, wasn't helping much either. It had taken Dante and Apollo the better part of an hour to get a fire going beyond a tiny, flickering flame that guttered and went out rapidly. It also meant that they were able to hear Dante curse everything from the fire to the jungle itself while they struggled. Dean had even heard Apollo chuckle a few times when Dante's frustration peaked.

The rest of them had left the duo to it while they attempted to set up camp as safely as possible. Dean knew enough about the jungle to know there were plenty of dangers hidden in the forest litter beneath their feet as much as in the forest canopy above them. The trick had been getting their makeshift shelters to protect them from above and below. Well, it had been a trick for Dean, and a bit tricky for Silun as well.

Dean had never learned how to rough it out in the wild and Silun's training had focused mainly on his shaman abilities. It had been up to Mikael and Katarina to help them each step of the way with erecting a temporary but relatively safe shelter.

"Ha! Fuck you jungle. Look at that!"

Dean turned at Dante's shout of victory to see a real fire burning up through the carefully arranged sticks they had found. If the fire took hold this time, they might be able to keep it going, even with the damp wood. At least, that's what he was hoping. He didn't actually know if the fire could burn hot enough to dry any fresh wood placed on it or not. Making a mental note to make sure he wasn't the one in charge of the fire, he smiled and turned back to setting up camp, as Dante continued to crow.

After making sure the fire had built nicely and would stay going, Apollo had borrowed the book about jungle flora and fauna from Dean. It wasn't the first time he'd taken it, having read it before they left, and on the plane. Dean had seen Apollo's ability to memorize information enough to know that the scout was just being cautious rather than trying to fill in any gaps in his knowledge. He hadn't asked, but he was betting that Apollo was checking the book's pages against whatever plants and animals they had seen along the way.

"So, we doing rations or are we gonna try to find something out there?" Katarina asked from her spot a safe distance away from the heat of the flames. Out of all of them, she was easily the one dealing with the sticky heat of the jungle with the least grace. All of them were miserable and hot, but despite all of her endurance skills, she seemed to be the most ill-equipped for the climate. She hadn't really stopped complaining about the heat, though after they entered the jungle, her complaints had been muttered under her breath.

"Dante and I will be going to get something soon. We need to keep the rations in case of emergency," Apollo told her distantly as he flipped through the pages.

"Wait, *we're* going out there huh?" Dante asked, slanting his eyes in Apollo's direction.

"Yes, we are," Apollo replied, sounding just as distant and unfazed as he had been with Katarina.

Nobody but Dean and Silun was paying attention to their conversation, having already tuned them out. Dean wasn't even sure Silun was paying attention to anything Apollo said, as his gaze was thoughtfully focused on Dante. It didn't take long to figure out what the shaman was thinking. On Dean's part, he wasn't used to seeing Apollo and Dante interact as constantly as they were now. Their trip into the mountains had involved conversation between them and Dean had glimpsed a small aspect of their relationship. Out here though, they lacked the need for subtlety and despite the foreign environment, the two of them were more at ease and willing to show a more casual side of themselves as they worked closely together.

"Are they always like that?" Dean asked Silun, who would have seen more of their interaction back in the Grove than Dean had.

Silun shook himself from his thoughts, smiling at Dean as the question sank in. "Who, Apollo and Dante? Yeah, they're always like that. Apollo doesn't really respond too much when Dante's like this. Drives Dante crazy and makes him want to act up even more to try to get a response out of him, even if it's just a smirk or something. I think Apollo knows it, so he does it on purpose to get a rise out of him."

Dean nodded in agreement, thinking of all the times he had seen an almost impish gleam in Apollo's eyes. Both the scout and the tracker had known each other for most, if not all, of their lives. Their respective jobs within the pack meant they probably worked together more often than they did with anyone else in their group. There was that edge of kinship between them that also lay between Katarina and Mikael, but the sort of casual almost playfulness that spoke of a relationship outside of something akin to family. It was more like two men with a deep respect for one another and who had been through a lot together.

Silun glanced from the two men, now eyeing the book together, and over to Kat and Mikael who were talking to one another on the opposite side of the fire, "Hey, Dean."

"Yes?"

"You gonna try to do your druid thing again while we're camped?"

Dean nodded. "Once it gets a little quieter around here, I planned to. Why?"

"That safe?"

"To be honest? I don't know. I wasn't really expecting the jungle to feel like it did and it still kind of feels like someone knocked me upside the head. I should have known better than to just try and dive into it and see what was around. It's a whole new environment for me and stopping to think about how much I should put out there would have been a more sensible first step."

Silun nodded in understanding, drifting off into his own thoughts once more. If there was one thing he could say about Silun's presence, it was that it was a comfort to know there was someone in their group who understood Dean when he started babbling on. It didn't often require too much explanation about Dean's abilities for Silun to understand most of what Dean was trying to say. Shamans and Druids might not operate in the same theater, but it seemed that they both understood the techniques involved.

"Have you tried?" Dean asked.

"Oh definitely," Silun chuckled. "And you're right it's...strange here."

"Strange how?"

"Well, it was a little like what you described when you tried earlier. There's like...a charge in the air. Like there's a spiritual, electrical storm just waiting to happen around here. And just like when there's a real lightning storm coming, it makes me want to get under cover, just in case. I haven't seen any spirits around here, not yet anyway, but there's definitely a lot of spiritual energy that fills this place."

Considering the amount of pure life energy that Dean had sensed, he could believe that. The physical and the spiritual realms were more tightly bound together than even the average werewolf knew. Dean had wondered if the spiritual element to this place was as charged as the physical was. In the past couple of months of talking to Silun, he had discovered that where he noticed something in the physical, there was also something similar or complementary in the spiritual. Where Dean had felt the pulse of life here as if it were a novalike power, Silun had sensed the potential for so much more.

"Potential," Dean mused aloud, liking the concept as soon as it had sprung into his mind.

Silun glanced at him questioningly. His brow was furrowed in thought and he glanced to where Dean had motioned. It had become a game to them over the past couple of months. They had walked and explored different areas around Dean's farm and the Grove and when they discovered a synchronicity between what both of them could sense, they had begun to wonder what the connection was in different locations. Whenever one of them felt they had figured out the connection, they would voice it aloud in the most concise and accurate way they could. It was then up to the other person to figure out their meaning, taking as long as they needed to before replying.

It had been Silun's idea, but Dean had taken to it quickly. Their powers didn't work on a logical level and required a great deal of intuitive and out of the box thinking. By having to work around a concise though vague concept presented by another, it allowed them to explore the nuances of their senses. Dean thought it was similar to the concept of koans, the esoteric riddles used by Zen Buddhists to expand the mind and provoke enlightenment. He had never bothered with that sort of thing before, but it had been doing wonders to help them understand their respective senses and abilities better.

"Yeah, it's not just life, is it?" Silun asked after a few minutes of thinking it over.

"For me it is. Almost too much of it."

Silun nodded once more, lapsing back into silence. He didn't look like he was going to argue with the idea and Dean felt pleased with himself. Their game was by no means a competitive one, but that didn't mean he didn't enjoy figuring out the answer before Silun did. Then again, he always enjoyed that eureka moment when Silun had reached the answer before he did. For Dean, it really was just the moment of sudden clarity that he enjoyed.

On a whim, Dean reached out with his senses to the jungle around them. This time, he was careful, only a sliver of his awareness tentatively pushing out of him. Even that minute amount had him wincing as the energy around them tried to rush in. It was so different from the patient manner of the forests back home. This energy demanded to be noticed and it was eager to fill every seemingly empty place that it could.

It was creation, but without the checks and balances, with nothing to keep it in line. The concept should have been wonderful and inspiring, but the reality was harsh and jagged. There was no real rhyme or reason to this place, only a hunger for more. Everything around them seemed to want to grow everywhere and anywhere, to dig deep into the earth and spread out further than it should. If the power within the crystals or within Nox had been entropy and death without control, then this place seemed to be creation and life without the same control.

"It's uncomfortable, isn't it?" Silun's voice broke through his thoughts, jarring him.

Dean shook his head, trying to rid himself of the frenetic energy. It didn't want to be driven from his mind any more than vines wanted to be pulled from where they so stubbornly clung. And just like vines, it felt like the energy here would choke the life from him if he didn't find some way to keep it in check.

"Dangerous," Dean replied finally, still feeling the echoes of the jungle in his mind.

"It doesn't feel like there's any one place where it's focused either. At least, not for me. Every nook and cranny of this place feels like it's filled with that spiritual electricity."

Dean glanced at him in worry. "Does that mean you can't sense where we're supposed to be going?"

Silun winced. "Sorry, Dean, but no. I could try to sense further if I wanted but..."

"But you don't want to be struck by lightning."

Silun nodded. "I can't tell if there's anything out there or if it's all like this. I mean, it's possible for a strong enough shaman to make pacts with spirits and influence their behavior. Enough spirits could make a place feel like this."

"But why?"

"To hide something? You said there's a chance there are people here with a lot of the answers you're looking for, right? That sounds like the type of people who want to hide themselves away from the world and not be found."

Dean grunted in agreement, unsurprised by Silun's answer. He hadn't expected it would be as easy as dragging a shaman here and magically finding the answer. What he'd read in Damian's journal made it sound like it would be hard to find the place. Nox had probably had to work hard to find it, or at least harder than simply walking in and knowing where to go. They were working off more information than Nox was, plotting the course that he had diligently traveled before them.

"Shitty rutters though," Dean said aloud.

"What's a rutter?" Silun asked.

"Old term used by sailors. Before there were charts, ships relied on the detailed journals written by the ship's pilots to get places. They were called rutters and they were the most vital thing a ship could have to get where they needed to go. The rutter would detail what a pilot saw along the way, so that someone else could travel the same path using those landmarks. It's a bit like what we're doing here, but Nox was pretty vague in a lot of his descriptions. Probably wrote down enough that he would remember when he read them, but not enough that someone else could easily walk the same path."

Silun blinked. "How do you know that sort of thing?"

Dean shrugged. "I read a lot. It was all I really had left when I lived in the city."

"Do you ever miss it?"

Dean looked startled. "What? Living by myself? Working a soul-deadening job and wondering if that was going to be my life forever? Lord no, not for a second have I missed it."

"Even if it was safer?"

He couldn't help but laugh at that. "Okay, maybe it was safer. A *lot* safer. In the last year, I've almost died more times than all the previous years combined. Yeah, there's been a lot of bad things that have happened to me, or that I've done, can't lie about that. But you know what, I wouldn't trade the life I have now for anything. I love working on the farm, it gives me a sense of purpose I never had before. And I have the love of a man who I never once would have thought I'd ever get the chance of meeting, let alone be tied to like I am. I have a family now, along with all the great and also irritating things that come with that."

"So, what you're saying is, you wouldn't do it because your life is better now?"

Dean shrugged, "I don't know if I'd call it better. It's better in many ways, and worse in others. I believe the good outweighs the bad, but even if it didn't, I don't think I would change anything. My life is the way it is because I made it that way. Because I chose it. I lived so much of my life before based on what I thought I should do, not on what I wanted to do. Now I'm living my life in the way my younger self always swore he would do: on my own terms. It might not be a perfect life, but I'm living it for myself, by my standards and rules. If that means inviting some extra hell into my life every now and then, so be it."

Silun was smiling at him, his expression a little sad. "You remind me of my master."

"I do?" Dean asked, feeling a little embarrassed that he had gone off on a tirade again.

"Yeah, she always said I was lucky to have found out I was a werewolf and then a shaman. She said it meant I was able to live my life in a way that so many others, including werewolves, never would. That despite all of my new responsibilities, I was more free than most of the people in my pack. That it might not feel like a choice on my part, but it was the most liberating choice of all."

Dean frowned. "What about that is liberating?"

Silun grinned. "The choice of being true to who and what you are."

At that, Dean returned his grin. "Sounds like a wise woman."

Silun nodded. "She was. I miss her a lot some days."

Familiar with the feeling, Dean looked away with a nod. "I'm sorry."

"Don't be. You didn't take her from me. Hell, you guys are the reason the person responsible for her death isn't around to do it to anyone else. I didn't tell you all that to make you feel bad. You know that, right? You just remind me of her sometimes."

Dean glanced back at Silun, a wry smile on his face. "Only sometimes?"

Silun laughed. "Yeah, like when you go off on one of your rants. She used to do that too. She was one hell of a woman. Didn't take anyone's crap and didn't apologize for being who she was. You're a lot like her, but I can't tell if you two would have liked each other or just fought all the time."

He thought about that before shrugging. "Hard to say,

but I do know it's a pity I never got the chance to meet her. She sounds like she was amazing, as well as wise."

Silun reached out and patted Dean's knee affectionately. "She was, but it's okay. I lost her, but I gained you and the rest of the pack. Like you said, things might be different now, but that doesn't make them better. No matter what happens, I know I have you guys and that makes all the difference in the world. Doesn't it?"

CHAPTER 12

"So, that counts as mountains around here?" Dante asked skeptically as he stared at the rise of land the river descended from.

"I never said it was mountains, only obviously elevated land," Dean pointed out.

Not that the land had been smooth to begin with. Even if it wasn't for the fact that the jungle was so overgrown it felt like it was actively fighting their every other step, there was still the land to contend with. It had dipped and risen seemingly without any rhyme or reason. Yet, it wasn't nearly as elevated as the land that now stood before them. It was definitely no mountain range, but it was much higher than the surrounding area.

"Okay. Well if this is the 'elevated' land that you're looking for, where do we go next?"

Dean could actually hear the quotes put around the word elevated. He had dealt with Dante enough to know that the man wasn't being as snarky as he sounded. When it came to Dante, when he was being sarcastic or swearing a lot, you were okay. It was when he started brooding quietly by himself that you had to watch out. Honestly, he and Apollo seemed the least affected by the climate, even if they were as red-faced and sweat soaked as the rest of them.

"Let me double-check everything and get my bearings. I don't want us to end up somewhere we're not supposed to be."

"Does in the middle of the jungle, with no idea where we're at count as where we're not supposed to be?" Dante asked, now smirking at Dean.

Refusing to take the bait, Dean shook his head lightly and pulled the map from his bag. If he was reading the compass right, they hadn't veered too much off the intended path. He thought that should be a good thing, but somehow the idea that everything was going right for them so far made him uneasy. It was paranoia, since the last mission he'd headed had gone to hell so quickly. It still made him twitchy.

"Alright, so we've been heading mostly north, following the river," he said aloud, the habit allowing him to think more clearly. "Which means, we need to head east from here."

"East to where?" Apollo asked, glancing in the direction they were meant to walk.

"There's apparently a grove of statues and flowers we need to find."

"Flowers," Dante said blandly.

"Dante, don't be an ass," Mikael grumbled at him, giving the cocky man a glare.

"What? I'm just saying that it's a little weird that it's flowers, so what?" Dante protested.

"What sort of flowers?" Apollo asked, not even bothering to pretend he wasn't ignoring the other two.

"Big ones. They 'make a rainbow' and smell like 'sugar-laced rotten meat'," Dean told him, quoting the journal he had brought with them.

Silun leaned over to read the journal. "That's pretty detailed for something you said was vague."

"Yeah, it gets a bit weird after that. If it wasn't for the fact that Nox was a shaman, I would have said he was high on something from the way he describes strange lights in the sky and smells that don't seem to really be there."

Silun raised a questioning brow, but added nothing else as he watched Dante and Mikael bicker. It was obvious to Dean that neither one of them was really feeling the argument, and they were just doing it to pass the time, or maybe amuse themselves. The only people Dante didn't have an almost aggressive relationship with were Silun and Apollo. Silun because he seemed to have a soft spot for the younger werewolf, and Apollo because, in Dean's opinion, it was next to impossible to be rude to the silent scout.

"You two are such children," Katarina huffed, fanning herself with a leaf she had plucked from somewhere.

"He started it," Mikael protested, belatedly realizing how childish the sentence sounded.

Dean shook his head at his mate, shooting him a small smile so he knew that he didn't mean it. Mikael had been on edge as much as Katarina had, though his nervousness manifested as an unusual silence, as opposed to her perpetual surliness. Dean hoped that whatever had taken over Mikael's frequent quiet moments wasn't going to be a problem. It wasn't like Mikael to keep something from Dean, at least not if it was something significant. He hoped they had moved beyond that.

"Well, now that we have that settled," Dean said with a repressed smile. "Maybe we can get moving?"

With more grumbling from Dante, they continued

moving deeper into the folds of the jungle. Dean had yet to risk reaching out with his senses again, but he would swear that the feeling of the jungle was growing stronger the deeper they went. There was nothing definite and it hadn't reached the levels it had with even the lightest brush of his senses. Still, he couldn't shake the feeling of oppressive power around him as they ventured further into the jungle. The headache he had developed the day before hadn't quite gone away just yet, sitting at the back of his head with a steady throb.

What he wanted was to ask Silun if maybe he was sensing anything as they moved deeper. However, that would lead to questions from the others; questions he wasn't quite ready to field. He appreciated their collective concern for his safety, but he didn't need them hovering over him like he might collapse from overextending himself at any point. That first taste of the kind of energy this jungle contained had been enough to keep caution at the forefront in his mind.

Silun himself was growing almost as quiet as Mikael as they traveled deeper. It irked Dean that he would have to wait until they had a quiet moment before he could question the young shaman. If Dean was noticing subtle changes in their environment over time, he would bet there were changes to whatever it was Silun was able to sense.

He suddenly realized that they had stopped, the whole group staring at him. Mikael looked at him with faint amusement and Dante was frowning at him in annoyance. The rest were staring at him with a mixture of confusion and slight concern. Belatedly, he realized that Dante had been talking to him from the front of their party and had asked him a question.

"Sorry," he said with a shrug. "What?"

Dante scoffed. "I asked how far we are gonna be traveling this time."

"Oh. I don't actually know. Damian didn't give even a hint of how long he traveled when he wrote down the descriptions. I'd say that we're gonna have to rely on your guys' werewolf senses to find the next place, but I'm betting the place with the statues and flowers will be easy to find. I get the feeling it has a strong enough smell to it that even I could find it."

"You're not gonna find anything if you keep going off into your own little world," Dante huffed, turning back around to continue leading them.

For the better part of the rest of the day, Dean did his best to keep himself from getting too distracted. It became increasingly difficult as their steady trek continued. The throb at the back of his head was growing stronger and his thoughts were growing harder to ignore. It was as if the energy of the jungle were infusing the power of his thoughts, making them as demanding and hungry to be acknowledged as the living things growing around him. He had never been so ill at ease with his own thoughts, nor had he ever felt as if he couldn't control his own mind. It was a disconcerting feeling and he was quickly becoming worried that he might end up being a hazard to this mission rather than a help.

Before he could finish the thought, a horrific smell hit him. It was overpowering enough that all rampant thoughts in his mind faded to the background the instant he registered the smell. His face scrunched up and he staggered as he tried to follow the others, coughing as he tried to cover his nose.

"Holy hell, that's awful," he groaned.

"Hasn't been any better for us for the past half a mile," Katarina groused from behind him.

Dean glanced back, and caught Mikael's eye, who simply shrugged. It hadn't occurred to him that they would have been smelling it for far longer than he had. He didn't know how they had tolerated it for so long, without even the slightest indication that they were smelling anything foul. Nox's description of the smell was appropriate, he would give the dead man that much. It was the equivalent of taking several rotting carcasses and drenching them in sickening sweet syrup and tossing rotted sugar on top.

He was bound and determined that if they could tolerate it, then so could he. The smell seemed to settle into his stomach and curdle as they walked onward. There was a faint hope that it might eventually become one of those smells you adjusted to, but he wasn't really betting on that happening. It was so pungent, he didn't think there was any way for his mind to shut it out and pretend it didn't exist.

"Silun? What is it?" Mikael's voice asked from behind him.

Dean turned to see the young werewolf staring into the distance, having stopped walking. His eyes danced as he watched the air before him. Silun's lips moved, as if he were speaking to himself.

"Silun?" Dean asked, stepping closer to him.

"There's something here."

Dean blinked at the response, turning around to stare in the direction Silun was looking. There was nothing there, but he felt the hairs on the back of his neck prickle. Ever since he had tried to connect with the jungle, he had felt a deep sense of unease that he hadn't been able to shake. Now Silun was talking about something else being there and it was doing nothing to ease Dean's nerves.

"A spirit?" he asked, hoping it was, and a friendly one at that.

Silun's face shifted to a soft smile. "A bunch of them."

From the way he was turning his head in multiple directions, Dean didn't think he was exaggerating. Everyone else had stopped, with Apollo and Dante talking at the head of their group. Katarina and Mikael had stepped back from Silun, leaving Dean to watch him silently. There was always a sense of understanding from everyone else whenever Dean or Silun did their thing. Dean supposed that just as he would never truly understand what it was like to be a werewolf, they knew they would never understand what being a druid or shaman meant.

Silun began speaking in a low voice, his words difficult to hear as he began to walk forward. Dean watched him, growing nervous again as Silun began to split from the group. It wasn't the first time he had seen Silun talk quietly to the air. It was the first time he had done it in the middle of a strange area, walking away from them as he appeared to talk to himself.

Finally, when Silun was a good distance away, Dean stirred, "Silun! Don't go too far, okay?"

The shaman didn't appear to hear him, continuing to walk forward with that vague smile still on his face. Something at the edge of Dean's senses piqued, drawing his attention. It wasn't a feeling that he could define precisely, but it felt like something shifted all around them. His eyes widened as he realized he was sensing the jungle's energies, even while refusing to open up his druidic senses. The strength of the jungle was escalating to the point that it didn't matter if he refused to see it or feel it, it was apparent to him all the same.

"Silun!" Dean called, now beginning to move toward the shaman.

Mikael grabbed his arm as Katarina moved forward with a huff. "I'll get him. Little idiot."

"Dean?" Mikael asked in a concerned voice, pulling him closer.

"Something's wrong Mikael," Dean said.

"How so?"

A gust of wind blew through the plants and trees around them, making them wince against the force of it. The sky darkened and Dean glanced up to see that it was now filled with dark clouds. Wind burst through the foliage once more, bringing with it the smell of ozone and rain.

"What the hell?" Mikael asked, looking up with a frown.

Dean glanced over at Apollo and Dante, then at Katarina who was still stomping after Silun, and his fear grew. "Hey! Don't separate!"

Before anyone could answer, there was a crack like an explosion from the sky above. Rain began to pour, falling in blinding sheets. Almost immediately, Dean could only see a few feet in front of him. There was a muffled shout of what could have been surprise or outrage from somewhere, but he couldn't tell who it was. The mixture of the rain pouring down and the constant cracks of thunder was drowning out his sense of distance.

"Dante! Apollo!" Dean called, trying to make his way to where he thought he had last seen them.

Mikael held tight to him, keeping pace with him as they tried to find the others. The sudden storm showed no signs of stopping. It was as violent as it was sudden, and it made the treacherous terrain all the more dangerous. The soaked ground and plants caused their feet to slip, slowing them more than their near-blindness already had.

Another crack of thunder, and the air around them filled with a blinding light. Heat slapped across Dean's face before what sounded like an explosion almost deafened him. He only had a moment to register the tree in front of them split in two before he heard Mikael shout in surprise from behind him. The hand at his elbow yanked backward, and he felt Mikael tumble. The two of them hit the ground, hitting the top of the slope they were on and tumbling down it with a chorus of shocked cries.

Plants slapped at his face as his body tumbled and rolled down the embankment. He didn't remember there being that big of an incline nearby. Either they had walked further through the storm than he thought they did or they had missed the hill that they were on. It felt like they tumbled for miles before they reached the bottom, Dean slamming into Mikael's prone body and flopping over him gracelessly, then rolling a bit further.

He spat out the mud that filled his mouth with a curse. "Mikael!"

"Here!"

If it wasn't for the fact that he could see the dim outline of his mate, the muffled sound would have made him think that Mikael was further away from him. Mikael was pushing up from the ground, checking himself over as best he could with water pouring down his face. He shook himself as he tried to help Dean up, who struggled to get out of the patch of thick mud that he had fallen into after rolling off Mikael.

"We have to find the others!" Dean yelled, having no other way to be heard over the sound of the ferocious storm.

"We can't! Not in this storm," Mikael shouted back.

Dean growled out another curse but nodded so that Mikael could see him. There was no way they would find anything in this storm. They couldn't see much more than a couple of feet in front of them and had to scream to be heard. Their chances of finding the others, especially after falling down as far as they had, were low.

"Shelter?" Dean yelled.

Mikael nodded vigorously as he turned around, probably in the hope of finding something that would serve as shelter for them. When he began to walk, Dean reached out and gripped onto his arm. Mikael looked back and smiled, looking water-soaked and handsome as he tried to lead them to what would count as a shelter.

CHAPTER 13

"Why is it always a cave?"

Mikael smiled softly at Dean's disgruntled question. "Because they're usually dry and defensible. Unless you want to try sleeping outside again."

Dean sighed, knowing he would rather face a night in another cave than try to fight the jungle and the storm again. Caves still weren't high on his list of favorite places to be, but it was better than out in the jungle. Most of the terror he felt when walking into a cave had been shed after everything had happened in the mines. Once he had wandered around in the dark, fought, and even killed in it, and then run from the collapse of the tunnels, he had lost the sharp edge of panic that caves had previously instilled in him.

"Aren't wolves den animals?" Dean asked as he stepped over the threshold dividing the cave from the outside.

"I feel like you're trying to make some sort of smartass comment."

"Was going to, but can't think of how to follow through on it."

They were ignoring the elephant in the room. Namely that they were separated from the others without any idea of how or where to find them. While looking for shelter, Dean had tried a couple of times to commune with the jungle, albeit cautiously. It had earned him the same results as his earlier attempts. In fact, it was even worse than before. If his senses were akin to sight, and the energies of the jungle were light, the whole place had gone supernova.

Mikael hadn't asked him about talking to the jungle. He either sensed that it wasn't working or maybe he could just tell that Dean was frustrated and confused. With daylight rapidly fading, they didn't have much choice but to find shelter and deal with finding the others in the morning. Trying to camp in the jungle had been dicey enough as it was. Dean didn't relish the idea of trying to hack his way through it in the dark.

"You still have that wood?" Mikael asked as he rummaged through his large backpack.

"It's all the dry wood we have for now, or the driest wood I have anyway. Hopefully the plastic held," Dean told him, swinging his own bag over his shoulder to set it next to Mikael's.

"Well, I'm willing to risk it. We can build a fire with the dry wood, and use the damper stuff we collected to keep it going after that. Should dry out in the fire fast enough without putting it out. Fire is going to have to be our best defense tonight."

Two exhausted people would make terrible guards. He knew that and he could feel rather than hear the worry in Mikael's voice as he rambled on. They were in a foreign environment without the support of the group to back them up. They were lost and the only person who could have been a feasible guide was Silun. That was, if he had managed to make better contact with a spirit than Dean had with the jungle.

"My plans always go to hell pretty early on, don't they?" Dean asked, realizing just how much trouble they were all in.

"I wouldn't go that far."

"Says the guy who didn't even want to be doing this in the first place."

"You know why, and plus, even if I were to say that your plans go to hell, at least they've always turned out good in the end."

"We're split up and lost in a jungle. I'm not seeing a good end to this."

"That's not your fault. How were you supposed to know there was a freak storm coming?"

Dean eyed him. "But I did, remember?"

Mikael went quiet then, focusing on the task of building the fire up. It left Dean to sit on a nearby rock and silently wonder how the others were doing. He hoped that he and Mikael had been the only ones split from the group. He didn't want to think about Silun somehow ending up wandering around the jungle on his own. Dean wouldn't forgive himself if something terrible happened to Silun because Dean had dragged him into this. It didn't matter that he had tried to make it Silun's choice, it had been Dean's idea, Dean's plan.

"You've got that look on your face again."

Dean looked up from the ground to meet Mikael's soft gaze. "The one that keeps making everyone worry about me?"

Mikael frowned. "Yeah, that one. You know it hurts to see that look on your face and know you won't let me help, right?"

Guilt made Dean look away. "I'm trying to not worry you."

"Bit late for that."

"I just," Dean began, struggling to find the words that would make Mikael understand. "I don't...I don't want to keep dealing with this. God Mikael, I killed three people during that last trip of ours and I don't know how to be okay with that. The wolf in the woods was self-defense, but that jailer, the one Silun called Scar? That wasn't self-defense, I provoked him, I pushed for him to come into the cage just so I could attack him. It wasn't self-defense or even me losing my mind on some fucker who enjoyed beating and cutting me for hours. I *planned* it. I made a conscious decision and I can...I still see all the blood when I'm asleep. I can taste it."

Mikael shifted closer to Dean, till he was kneeling between Dean's legs. "And the third?"

"What?" Dean asked, realizing too late what he had said.

"You said three, but all I know about is two, who was the third, Dean?"

It was said so quietly, so calmly, but Dean winced all the same. He didn't pull his hand away when Mikael reached for it. It was too late to take it back and he would need that comforting grip when as he fessed up. He had kept the little detail of why Damian had fallen into the crevice to himself. The only person he thought might have seen or suspected what had happened was Apollo. Neither of them had spoken of it, not until now anyway.

"Damian."

Mikael straightened a little. "I thought he fell?"

Dean took a deep breath to steady himself. "He did. When that crack opened up, he fell in but caught himself on my arm. I can still see the way he looked up at me as he hung there Mikael. He was terrified, almost out of his head with fear. And then I stabbed him. I found my knife and stabbed him to make him let go. And it wasn't because I was afraid he'd pull me in. I wanted him dead, Mikael. Dead and gone. So, I made sure he was."

With that, his momentum drained out of him and he went silent. Mikael knelt before him, hand still twined around his, gazing up at him with a thoughtful expression. Dean didn't know what he expected Mikael to do or say now that he had told him the truth. The rational part of him knew that Mikael wouldn't treat him badly. The emotional, fearful part of him however, was beginning to panic at Mikael's silence.

"You know, I wondered," Mikael finally said.

Dean drew back a little in surprise. "You did?"

Mikael smiled. "Yeah, I think it's the bond thing. I could tell that something was up every time you talked about Damian's death. I don't really know how to explain it, but it was like I could feel you...pull back, withdraw into yourself. And you didn't have to do that, Dean. You could have told me."

"I know and I should have. I didn't want to lie to you or not tell you the whole truth. It's just, even telling you now, it has my stomach twisted in knots. How I...I killed Scar, that was awful because of how messy it was, how violent and fucking unnecessary it was. But Damian? I wanted his death. I wanted him to fall into that pit and never come back up. No one else was there to do it and I was glad it was me. That's the worst part. Some part of me loved doing that."

"Dean," Mikael leaned in closer so their faces were only inches apart. "Of course you did. He tried to kill the people you care about, had you tortured for his own plans, and then kidnapped your friend and used him to power some death crystal. Wanting him dead is a pretty normal reaction."

"Wanting it and actually doing it are two different things, Mikael."

"Babe, you're not a bad person for that. He might not have been an immediate threat at that precise moment, but he was still a threat. And before you say it, it's not wrong that you enjoyed it, either. Anyone in your position would have, especially if they had gone through everything you did."

Dean bit his bottom lip, still not looking at Mikael. "Yeah."

"That doesn't sound very convincing. I'm not helping much here, am I?"

If he meant if he was making it seem what Dean had done was acceptable, then no. He knew if their positions were reversed, he wouldn't think any less of Mikael. Hell, Mikael probably wouldn't have been bothered in the slightest if he'd been the one to make the decision. That was just the kind of life in which he had been raised and Dean understood. That understanding did nothing to assuage his guilt, however. Knowing something logically didn't mean his heart understood or accepted it, or even wanted to.

Dean squeezed Mikael's fingers. "You always help, Mikael, just by being you. You've always got my back, and just telling you has...well, it hasn't made it better, but it makes it easier somehow. We're lost in some far-flung part of the world, stuck in a cave, and I'm admitting to murder, but everything feels a bit better because you're holding my hand while all of that happens."

Warmth flooded Mikael's face, his eyes brimming with love. "Good. That's all I can ask for."

Dean gave a watery chuckle. "I'm sorry I was such an

ass to you back at the Grove. You and everyone else have only been trying to make sure I'm okay. But instead of just owning up that I wasn't okay, I snapped at everyone, especially you. I should have been better than that."

"I probably could have phrased it better, and you know, not yelled at you over it. Can't exactly pull off patient compassion when you're yelling at the other person."

Dean leaned closer, kissing Mikael's forehead gently. "You yell because you care, baby."

"That is like, the least romantic sentence I think I have ever heard you say."

"So, kiss me before I try to top it."

With a fond smile on his face, Mikael leaned up to do just that. Dean could feel the smile still on Mikael's lips as they met his. Warmth that had nothing to do with the growing fire spread through him. He reached to grip onto Mikael's shoulders, pulling him closer. Mikael's body pressed firmly against him, long arms enfolding him.

Even with the heat of the jungle hanging around them, Dean still craved the warmth he could feel spilling out of Mikael. The raw emotion in his chest pounded with the same steady beat of his heart, his pulse jumping as Mikael's mouth slipped down the skin of his throat. Dean's gasp was soft as he felt the scrape of teeth along the sensitive flesh. Electricity sparked down his spine as the sharp edges of Mikael's teeth sank lightly into the scar on his shoulder from when Mikael had mated him.

He knew where this was heading, and he only had a moment to think about the fact that they were about to screw around in a cave again. The thought flew from his mind the moment Mikael's teeth dug deeper into the sensitive scar. Skilled fingers unsnapped the button of his pants, fingertips sliding his shirt up. Mikael's nails slid along

Dean's warm skin, drawing an eager breath from him as he waited to see if they would bite into his skin.

"Dean?" Mikael asked, reacting as he felt the sudden shift in Dean's need. Dean didn't remember the last time his need to experience Mikael's strength had been this urgent. His need to experience the hint of danger that Mikael could bring. His inner turmoil had flipped within him and he needed something more than light touches and sweet kisses.

"Tell me you have lube," Dean gasped, almost writhing. "I don't want to have to use spit but fucking hell, I need you inside me, Mikael."

The desire in Mikael's eyes was marred by surprise for a moment, but only a moment. He nodded, leaning back to yank his bag closer to them. Dean's eyes followed the bottle of lube eagerly, reaching his hand out for it. He finished the job of removing his pants and underwear with one hand as Mikael handed the bottle to him. Dean's eyes never left Mikael's, drinking in the rising lust as he stripped his lower half of his clothing.

Mikael scooted back as Dean knelt over his groin. A faint breeze blew across his bare skin as Dean worked to undo Mikael's pants. It was a bit of a struggle, freeing Mikael's cock from the confines of his jeans. He was rock hard already and that always made it tricky to safely pull him free. The silken skin of his shaft greeted Dean's touch.

"I love when you get this hard," Dean told him as he finally managed to pull Mikael's cock out into the open.

"Hard not to when you do this."

Dean guided Mikael's hands onto each side of his ass. "Hold me steady, okay?"

The lube was cool, as expected, and he slicked the both of them. Neither of them said a word as Dean got into position, holding onto Mikael's shoulders as he let himself slip down. At first, there was the expected resistance. No matter how often they slept together, there was always that initial fight when his muscles resisted the intrusion of Mikael pushing inside him. Then they gave as he jerked his hips down, crying out as he felt the thick head of Mikael's cock shove into him.

Knowing it wasn't the best idea, but not caring, Dean let himself fall further. Mikael's cock spread him open force-fully as he drove himself down. He would never have been able to manage this months ago, and even with all the prac-tice he'd had, it still burned. His back arched, pulse pounding in his throat as the burning pleasure throbbed where their bodies connected. He couldn't express all that was going on in his head as he'd told his story to Mikael, but he could find a way to ease the desperate need within him.

Below him, Mikael swore gutturally under his breath as Dean relentlessly sank down onto him. Strong fingers pressed against the flesh of Dean's ass, Mikael's nails biting into his skin. Mikael shuddered, arms shaking as they held Dean as steady as they could. For Dean, his hands were there to catch him if his legs threatened to give out. He wanted Mikael inside him as fast as possible, even though it burned and ached. However, it didn't mean he was so desperate that he was willing to thrust Mikael's entire length up into his ass all at once.

Dean's ass pressed against Mikael's thighs as he bottomed out, finally feeling the whole of Mikael inside him. The thought drew a low moan from Dean's throat as he pushed himself up. So long as he was moving, the pain felt like pleasure in his mind. Mikael's hands rose with him, holding tight as Dean impaled himself once more. The two of them cried out in unison, clinging to one another as they found their rhythm.

Mikael's hands slid up to grip Dean's waist, nails biting into a fresh patch of skin as Dean pulled him into the moment. The slap of skin as he pulled Dean down onto him was followed by another cry of pleasure from Dean. Dean's body felt as if it was vibrating as Mikael took the lead. His firm grip pulling Dean up only to immediately pull him back down. It was hard to keep his muscles from going limp as he held tight to Mikael's shoulders.

The sound of their coupling echoed off of the stone walls of the cave. Sweat dampened skin slid together as they moved as one. Dean's body seemed to come alive with nerve endings he didn't know he had. The pain was gone now; either that, or it had become indistinguishable from the pleasure jolting through him. Each push of Mikael's cock within him brought another sudden flood of ecstasy. Neither of them had words, but their intense gazes were locked on each other.

Dean's cock was sandwiched between the two of them as Mikael thrust Dean's body up and down. It made a mess, leaking profusely with each downward motion. There was no reaching between the two of them to grab hold of himself either. There was no room for his hand and he didn't dare interrupt the harsh rhythm they had created.

The muscles in his body surged to life, heat flaring from the tips of his toes and rushing headlong to his groin. With an almighty cry, he shoved himself down as his orgasm erupted from him. His nails dug deep into the skin of Mikael's shoulders as his cock exploded between them. His cries mingled with Mikael's, feeling the thickness within him swell as Mikael unloaded deep within him. The sound of their shared orgasm seemed deafening to Dean's ears, but it was one of the greatest, most erotic sounds he had ever heard.

With the suddenness of a light going out, the ecstasy and the strength of his body were gone. He slumped forward, burying his face in the crook of Mikael's shoulder. Mikael's grip on his waist shifted, his arms wrapping themselves around Dean instead. The cock deep inside of him still moved slightly causing Dean to moan pitifully. Uncomfortably bright flashes of sensation pulsed through him, but he didn't have the strength or inclination to put an end to it.

For a moment, all they could do was cling onto one another, trying to recover both strength and breath. Bit by bit, Dean felt his heart slow, easing from the pounding in his chest to a far more comfortable and steady thump. Mikael shifted below him, raising both of them up so that he slipped free from Dean. There was no helping the little gasp that escaped as he felt Mikael pull out, leaving behind a tender and empty feeling within him.

Gaining some measure of his strength back, Dean managed to sit himself beside Mikael, leaning against the rock he had been sitting on earlier. They lay their heads together, their fingers tracing lazy patterns on one another's skin. Dean could see the evidence of his orgasm on both their chests and stomachs, mingling with droplets of sweat. Mikael's was no longer deep inside him, but Dean felt so hypersensitive at that moment he thought he could almost still feel him.

Intimacy was one thing that came easily to the both of them. The sex had been exhilarating and intimate in its implicit trust and respect. But even that paled in comparison to the intimacy they shared as they sat shoulder to shoulder against the stone wall of the cave. They weren't wrapped around one another, gazing into one another's eyes, or speaking sweet nothings to each other. They were leaned against one another, as Dean was thinking about the load inside him and on his stomach, and the ache he would probably have come morning. He was thinking how he never wanted anyone else's semen in him, not when he had the one person who understood him better than he understood himself to fill him up.

He had the pain as much as the pleasure and Mikael had given it to him. Not just as a gift to Dean, but it was something Mikael wanted to do as well. If Dean thought about it, it was cathartic for them both. The inner struggle that Dean found difficult to express, had a means of release. It was something he could ask of Mikael without fear of judgment or concern. In turn, he knew that some primal part of Mikael thrived on those rare moments when Dean tossed caution to the wind. It took their passionate sex and drove it into those primal realms that Mikael's animal craved.

"That help?" Mikael asked finally, voice sounding rough as he nuzzled against Dean's temple.

"Yeah, but some food would be great, too."

"You're such a man."

CHAPTER 14

There was no way around it; they were definitely lost in the middle of the jungle. Neither of them were expert trackers and they couldn't rely on previous knowledge to get them through this. Dean couldn't even rely on his normal druid senses to help them navigate through their surroundings, which was growing more and more frustrating for him. The storm might have passed, but the jungle was as difficult to commune with as it was before.

When they woke up, the storm was over. They started the day by trying to find the hill they had rolled down. After a few hours of getting stuck in mud several times, fighting off a few dozen insects and snakes, and almost losing Mikael down a random sinkhole, Dean had just about had enough. He was fed up with this little trip. They were hot, under attack from the wildlife, separated from their friends, and hopelessly lost.

"Save the fucking rainforest," Dean groused, smacking at another huge bug as it landed on his exposed neck.

Mikael chuckled, reaching out to rub Dean's upper arm as they walked. Dean could tell that them being lost wasn't helping Mikael's mood any more than his. Yet, his mate was doing a better job at keeping his head up and trying to soldier through it than he was. Dean's mood felt like it was as sour as Katarina's had been the last time he'd seen her. He seriously hoped she was alright and that she had managed to get to Silun before the storm hit too hard. He hated the idea of everyone being split up, but if they were at least in groups of two, that was better than wandering around this hateful place alone.

"I'm hungry," Dean complained, hating the frustrated whine he could hear in his voice.

"Mmm, so am I. Think that's safe to eat?" Mikael asked, pointing at a nearby plant with what looked like several colorful berries on it.

"Don't know. Apollo has my book. Could be safe or we could die from some horrible poison that's in them."

Mikael eyed him with a smile. "Aren't we perky?"

Dean rolled his eyes, but begrudgingly returned the smile. It wouldn't do for him to be stomping around in a grumpy mood. Both of them were in this together, and he didn't want to be the one to bring the mood down further than it already was. Well, that and it was nearly impossible to be angry when Mikael smiled at him like that. The ache of his body, coupled with the release of having cleansed himself of his secret made him feel a bit better.

"Unless we see a banana or something we know, I think we should stick to our rations," Dean offered up, pleased that his tone sounded less moody.

"How do you think monkey tastes?"

Dean looked up to eye the creatures swinging through the trees over their heads. The animals had been keeping pace with them ever since they left the cave. He didn't want to sound paranoid and say they were following them, but he thought it was a strange way to behave nevertheless. He knew enough about monkeys to know they were curious creatures, but it seemed odd that they would have followed them for this long. Not once had the monkeys allowed Dean or Mikael out of their sight, but they always stayed out of range to them.

"If you want to climb up there and try to get hold of one, be my guest," Dean told him, squinting up at the animals.

"Pretty sure that's a fight that I would lose and I really don't want 'killed by monkeys in a tree' on my gravestone."

Dean snorted, shaking his head as they continued to walk. The morning had slipped into late afternoon and they still had no idea where they, or the others, were. He wasn't as concerned about Apollo and Dante. If they had stuck together, they would have a fighting chance. The two of them together were a formidable duo, even in an environment they had no experience of. If Katarina stayed with Silun, he bet they would be safe too. If only because he was sure she could win a fight between her and a pack of monkeys if she wanted to.

"Ya know, I bet Silun is going to find the place you were looking for," Mikael said suddenly.

"What makes you say that?"

"Didn't you say something about how Nox had used the spirits of the jungle to find his way once he got to a certain point? Kinda seemed like that's what Silun was seeing before the storm hit, don't ya think?"

Actually, Dean hadn't given that particular detail much thought. He thought it wasn't a coincidence that Silun started seeing spirits and talking to them, only for that powerful storm to hit right at the same time. Yet, he hadn't given it any thought beyond the two events being connected, or that it might actually be exactly what they needed.

"Guess that works for my whole 'the storm wasn't an accident' theory," Dean said.

"Didn't think so either, huh?"

Dean shook his head. "Silun finally meets some spirits and starts talking to them, then suddenly a storm? I'm not a big believer in coincidence. Especially when right before the storm hit, the jungle felt...weird."

"Yeah, but you said it already felt weird before that, so what was different?"

"I could feel its energies all of a sudden," Dean explained, swatting away a cloud of insects.

"Okay, but how is that any different from any other time you've sensed the energies of a place?"

"Because I wasn't using my senses, but the jungle was so...amped up I could feel it anyway. It's like closing your eyes, but still being blinded by a light."

Mikael thought about that for a minute. "So, Silun sees spirits for the first time since he got here and was able to talk to them. Then you suddenly feel the jungle doing something, or getting excited or whatever, even though you weren't even trying to listen. Then a storm hits out of nowhere, separating the six of us so we can't find each other even now. That's about it?"

Dean nodded. "Seems like an accurate summary of our current predicament, yes."

"So, what's the running theory? You think the jungle caused it?"

"I don't know. Last I checked, the only people who can influence a forest or jungle, or whatever, are druids. And supposedly, I'm the last druid, as far as we know anyway.

Plus, even with all the stuff that I've done, I've never been able to cause a storm before."

"You caused the mountain to go all earthquakey," Mikael pointed out.

"Yeah, but that was the mountain. It had a mind and a soul, or something like that. That's different, it's not the same thing as a storm. A mountain might quake, but a jungle or forest doesn't cause a storm."

"So, why is the jungle going all wild in your senses?"

Dean could only shrug once more. "Maybe they're connected? Like, whatever brought the storm about is somehow tied to the jungle too? I mean, I guess a strong enough spirit could cause it, or many spirits working together. And spirits are tied to the place they're in. So, it's possible that it was a spirit, or spirits, that made it happen and the jungle just responded to the increase in spiritual activity."

"That would mean it could have been a shaman, right?"

"I guess it would depend on how strong the shaman was and how close they are to the spirits. I mean, someone who lived here their whole life would be really close to the spirits of this place I'm sure. But why?"

Mikael motioned around them. "To separate us like it did?"

When Dean had read in the notes that there had been hostile locals around here, he hadn't expected they would use the weather against them. It was only a theory, but it certainly sounded right to him. There had only been that brief surge of power and then the storm had come crashing down around them. He didn't think that was an accident, but he marveled at the amount of power it would have required to do that.

"Okay," Dean began, continuing with the theory that it

was intentional. "Say that was the aim. Why separate us and then do nothing afterwards? You and I have been wandering about for hours now and the only thing we've been attacked by is some hungry bugs."

Mikael opened his mouth to respond and then froze. His mouth slammed shut, jaw tightening as he swiveled his head around. Dean knew he was listening to something that he himself couldn't hear and he kept silent. Mikael's shoulders bunched as his eyes began to shift with different colors. Whatever he was hearing, it was enough to warrant him being willing to turn wolf.

"Oh hell, don't tell me that we're about to get the answer to my question," Dean griped, wishing he had focused on his fighting lessons a little better now.

Patches of fur began to show on Mikael's body as he let the change take hold of him. He pushed against his clothes, Dean hastily catching them so that they weren't lost. Mikael's head never stopped moving around as he tried to find the source of whatever it was he had heard. Dean's frustration at his inability to talk to the jungle, to be able to get some sort of information about what might be out there, grew as he gathered up Mikael's shoes.

The two of them stood there, waiting for the threat to approach. All Dean could hear were the normal sounds of the jungle and the low warning rumble in Mikael's throat. His muscles were bunched up as he readied himself for the attack, anxious to get to the fight. Dean had known there was a possibility of a fight, but he had hoped it would be when the others were around. They were down three fighters, since he wasn't exactly the most reliable in a fight. He had survived his last encounters because he either had more back-up, the element of surprise, or sheer luck.

"Babe, you sure you heard something?" Dean asked as he continued to look around, seeing only the jungle.

Mikael snarled as an arrow hissed past them, burying itself in the ground at Dean's feet. Dean yelped in surprise, dancing back from the arrow and looking in the direction it had come from. There was nothing there, but a bunch of plants and trees. Another arrow drove into the wood of the tree beside him, the shaft still quivering as it vibrated less than an inch from his nose.

He heard more hissing as Mikael bounded forward into the brush, disappearing beneath the thick canopy of flora. Dean scrambled away as the arrows drove into the mud around him, never quite hitting him. He didn't know if he was just getting lucky or if their attackers were intentionally missing him. Dean hoped it was the latter because he did not want to be hit with a few arrows if his luck decided to run out.

Dean saw movement out of the corner of his eye and he reacted swiftly. The strange man only had a moment to think before Dean tackled him, driving them both to the ground. The man's bow, complete with nocked arrow, went flying into the thick foliage. Shocked that he had managed to catch him by surprise, Dean followed through by driving his fist into the man's jaw. Pain lit up his arm, making him shake his hand as the man's head bounced off the ground. He was only dazed but it was enough for Dean to grab hold of his head and thump it back down again until he saw the man's eyes roll up and his body go still.

Another flash of movement to the side and he immediately lashed out with a harsh kick. This stranger was quicker, moving out of Dean's reach with a graceful side step. Before he could nock another arrow, Dean rolled toward him and lashed out again. His only hope was to keep his opponent off balance. During their training, Katarina had praised him on being willing to be aggressive, despite his low skill. According to her, it was a good way to keep all but the most highly trained and hardened opponents off-balance. He had been skeptical before but now, he was beginning to see the sense behind it.

The man dodged him again, but Dean's foot snagged in the lower arch of the bow, ripping it from his grasp. Even now, he could hear the shouts and snarls from somewhere behind them. There were more than just these two, and from the number of voices he was hearing, he was betting that he and Mikael had their hands full.

Pain lanced up his side as the man sidestepped and drove his foot into Dean. The guy was wearing what looked like handmade leather shoes. Not the thick-soled leather shoes Dean would have expected, but more like wraps made of leather, around each foot. Enough to protect his feet against the elements, without weighing the man down or making it difficult to be stealthy. The stranger didn't have much else in the way of clothing either, only body paint that Dean imagined was supposed to work as camouflage.

Dean reared up, driving his head into the man's gut and shoving him away. His side still ached as he launched himself once more. The guy wasn't quick enough this time, and they both fell to the ground. A fist lashed out, slamming into Dean's head but he ignored the throbbing pain as he tried to strike back. The man said something harshly in a tongue Dean didn't understand, but from the tone, he would bet the man wasn't calling him anything pleasant.

"Yeah? Screw you too," Dean hissed back as he punched the man across the jaw, not caring this time how much it hurt. All his frustrations at being lost and separated were coming to the fore. The violence and even the pain were exciting, and he struck again, hearing the man grunt in pain and surprise.

As he raised his fist to strike one more time, that strange lilting language called out through the jungle air. He had no idea what was said, but he knew when he was being called out. Before he could decide whether to finish knocking the second stranger out or not, a sharp yelp pierced the air.

Dean was on his feet instantly, hand going to his side, eyes searching for Mikael. He found him on the ground, almost completely circled by half a dozen people, both men and women, dressed in similar fashion to the two Dean had been fighting. One of them, a large man who appeared to be about Samuel's age, stood in front of the group, facing Dean.

It was obvious the sheer numbers had overwhelmed Mikael, who lay on the ground, panting and bleeding from a few places. There were what appeared to be spears pointed at him as he lay there. Dean could see the glint of pointed tips and recognized they were crafted from silver. They were dealing with people who knew what they were and how to fight them, great.

The man at the front, the one Dean thought of as the leader, raised a single brow at him. It was a look of question and Dean shrugged in response, motioning to the two on the ground behind him. The leader nodded, smiling slightly as he similarly motioned to Mikael, now with a look of expectation.

Dean would have laughed, if he wasn't feeling so frustrated. Of course he had no choice but to give up. They had him totally outnumbered and effectively had Mikael held hostage. Since they hadn't actually killed Mikael and had missed every shot at Dean, he didn't think they were here to kill them. All he could hope was they were here to escort them to wherever they had come from.

Slowly, Dean raised his hands in the air above his head, palms outward. The two not holding silver tipped spears over Mikael came forward. The woman grabbed his arms and forced them down behind his back roughly enough to make Dean hiss in pain. He felt the rough rasp of rope against his wrists as she bound them together. She hissed something angrily at him as the man who had come with her bent to check on the two men Dean had been fighting.

The one Dean had been ready to knock out was already sitting up, murmuring quietly to his friend. The other was beginning to stir, already shaking off the blows to his head and coming slowly back to consciousness. The man who had come to check on them jabbed the barely moving one with his toe, barking something at him as he awoke. They had a short conversation and the standing stranger laughed quietly, mocking.

"Alright, alright," Dean hissed as the woman shoved him forward toward the rest of the group.

As he approached, he saw that all of them, save for the leader, were sporting wounds of their own. Mikael might have been outnumbered and eventually overwhelmed, but he had put up one hell of a fight. One of them had a bloody cloth wrapped around his upper arm and another was holding a hand to his neck. None of the wounds looked fatal, but Mikael had done a number on them. He could only imagine how it would have gone if all of their group had been there to fight.

"So, where to?" Dean asked the leader, knowing that the guy couldn't understand him.

The leader grinned. It was the last thing Dean saw clearly as a dark sack was shoved over his head.

CHAPTER 15

"I s this your idea of hospitality?" Dean shouted, hearing his voice echo off the stone walls around him.

No answer came back to him, not that he expected one. The tribal people led them through the jungle, with Dean blindfolded. He expected that they had found a way to blindfold Mikael as well, but Dean hadn't actually seen it. None of them had answered any of his questions or even bothered to respond to his comments. They silently led them both to wherever they were now.

At least, he hoped Mikael was somewhere nearby. When they finally removed the sack from his head, all he could see was the stone walls he saw now. The coolness of the stone was a relief from the oppressive heat of the jungle and the smell of dust and earth wasn't unpleasant. There was nowhere comfortable for him to lay or sit, as even the floor was stone. Still, considering the accommodations of the last two times he had been held prisoner, he couldn't complain. At least no one had showed up to start torturing him, yet.

He attempted to keep track of where they were going, but it had proven fruitless. He didn't know this land any more than these people would have known the forest around the Grove. They had walked for hours until they reached this place. He didn't even know how long he had been in this cell, only that it felt like days. It hadn't been days, but time passed differently when you were imprisoned. No light reached the cell he was in, so he couldn't tell what time of day it was. He could only mark the few occasions food had been brought to him.

If he were to take a guess, he would say it had taken the remaining daylight for them to reach this place. After that, he could only guess that he had been in the cell for a day or two. They had taken all of their things and Dean had nothing but his own thoughts to keep him company. The only interaction he'd received so far was when they brought him his meals. Even then, the people who brought his food were silent and couldn't be persuaded to do more than set his food down and leave.

He toed the earthenware bowl his last meal had been brought in. The food had been simple, but fresh. They certainly weren't sending him gruel or hard tack and bread. If he were honest, the food was better than the rations he and Mikael would have had to survive on. He only hoped that wherever Mikael was, he was being treated well.

When the door's thick lock gave way, Dean barely stirred. He had given up trying to get someone to acknowledge him at this point. It hadn't been long enough for him to have lost hope, but he felt he was smart enough to know a losing battle when he saw one. When they wanted something from him, that's when they would talk to him.

The figure entered the room and loomed over him. A leather covered foot reached out and poked at his side to get his attention. That soft language breathed out of the woman who stood over him, getting his attention as much as the foot. He looked up, unable to make out her face in the gloom of the cell.

"What?" Dean asked belligerently, knowing she couldn't answer him.

She motioned for him to follow her, stepping back toward the door to give him space. Even if it was what Dean had been hoping would happen, he heaved himself up with some reluctance. It had seemed easy just to wait for them to want to talk to him, but now that they did, his heart had begun to hammer.

"Don't know what good it will do, since we can't exactly talk," Dean told her as he followed her out. She was small, almost as small as Lucille was. Yet, her dark eyes spoke of the same playful danger that Katarina had about her. Two blades sat sheathed at her hips and he was amused to see that she was utterly topless. She caught him looking at her chest and smirked, before leading him out.

The cell opened up into a hallway formed entirely of stone. The stairs were the same and their footsteps echoed as they climbed up around another bend. At the end of that hallway lay a thick door, like the one on his cell. The walls of the hallway were etched with various looping symbols and figures. He couldn't tell if there was a story being told there or if everything was just random, but his escort never faltered and he didn't want to risk what might happen if he fell behind.

When the door opened, it was into blinding sun. He winced against the light, still trying to keep up with the woman's quick pace. They were on a structure that was raised above the thick foliage of the jungle. As he followed, he glanced over the side of the stone walkway they were on, seeing the ground a few stories below them.

He glanced all around as they walked, trying to take in the place. It was almost like a temple, though solid, like a fortress. She turned to lead him up a wide set of stairs that extended to the top of the building and all the way down to jungle level. The top of the stairs opened up into a large courtyard. Time had aged the stone around them, as it had everywhere else, but it was still beautiful. A clear pool of water sat in an etched square at the center and plant life flourished in various places around the water and walls. Only the pool was laid out in a specific way. The plants sprawled all over the place save for designated paths on each side.

"Wow, it's beautiful," he told the woman in awe, not caring that she couldn't understand him.

"I am glad you think so," an accented female voice said from near the pool of water.

Startled, both at the sudden voice and at the sound of English, Dean paused. A woman knelt by the pool, then stood slowly as she appraised Dean. Her hair was pure silver, long, and plaited behind her to lay against her back. She was slight, but held herself with a great deal of confidence and strength. Dean noticed that her eyes were two different colors, one as green as the plants around her, and the other yellow, flecked with the same color as the green eye.

"Dean, yes?" she asked, her voice firm but holding that same lilt from the language he had heard the others speak.

"I, yeah, and you are?" he asked, already feeling off-balance.

"In this place, we do not have names. We have titles and

those are the names we go by," she explained as she ran her fingers over the petals of a large flower.

"Okay, then what would your title be?"

She smiled at that. "I am referred to as the Watcher."

He didn't quite know how to respond to that, so he moved on, "Okay, so how did you know my name?"

"We have been watching you and your friends for quite some time. We have the means to keep an eye on you without you knowing it. It is one of the many gifts that we are afforded here."

Dean thought back and snorted, "The monkeys?"

"That is one way, though perhaps not in the way you might think."

Dean thought again. "There are spirits, tied in some way to the monkeys, that you can communicate with."

She raised her brow slightly. "Well, perhaps it is in the way you might think. You are not one of ours, so you could not be a shaman to know that. Your friendship with the other, perhaps?"

Dean hesitated, wondering how much he should tell this woman. Save for the woman who had escorted him here, she was alone with him. There wasn't a great deal of threat to him at the moment, but he held back all the same. Him being a druid had caused plenty of problems in the past. He didn't want to risk putting him or the others in greater danger than they already were, without knowing more.

"So, you've seen Silun then? Is he okay?" Dean asked, hoping to get some sort of news about the others.

"Oh, yes, they'll be fine. The young shaman and the woman with him are here as well."

Dean perked up at that. "She was with him? Oh thank God, I was worried."

She watched him carefully as she spoke. "Yes, we gathered them up before we got to you. The woman, put up quite a fight. No one was killed, but we will have to see if one of ours will ever have complete use of their arm."

Dean winced at that, but shifted to a frown. "Wait, 'gathered us?' Seems like a nice way of saying that you took us prisoner and locked us up."

"I'm sure that's how it seems to you, but remember, you are the intruders here. We aren't prone to allowing trespassers around here, particularly those who are here for a purpose. From the moment you stepped into our home, you have been searching for something."

"There are ruins all over the place around here. How does looking for a bit of adventure warrant us being locked up?" Dean asked, trying to skirt around the truth.

She laughed. "You are aware that I can read as well as speak your tongue, yes? And that I did go through your belongings after we took them off you?"

Dean frowned, though he wasn't surprised to hear that. He hadn't given a thought to his things being taken except that it was everything he needed to survive out in the jungle. Now there was the added and unexpected snare of this woman having been able to go through everything. From her words, he guessed that meant she had gone through the journal he had brought with him.

"You've read Damian's journal," he stated plainly.

"I did. And it would do you well to simply be honest with me, Dean. We appreciate that around here."

Dean crossed his arms across his chest. "Forgive me if I'm a bit hesitant about sharing any and all information with the people who showed up shooting arrows at us and then kidnapped us. Oh, and I'm pretty sure you're the reason we all got separated from one another too."

She only smiled, turning to prune the plants near her. "This Damian, he sounds...interesting."

"He was, if that's what you want to call it," Dean told her, gritting his teeth.

"Dead, is he? Good. Men like that are dangerous when they're left alive for too long. Even that little bit I read told me he was arrogant, devious, and hungry for more power than he should have wanted. Ambition left unchecked is a poison, often a lethal one."

"Proved lethal for him. I take it you read the parts that he took from Nox's journal then?"

Her face darkened at the mention of the fallen shaman's name. "That was not the name he went by when he came here, under the guise of friendship."

Dean glanced at the younger woman who stood a fair distance away. She had a faraway look, as if she weren't paying the slightest bit of attention to the conversation going on in front of her. Dean didn't know if she could understand anything that they were saying, but he knew she was more attentive than she appeared. He had no doubt that the older woman could hold her own, but the weapons on the young woman's hips told him she was here in case he decided to get violent.

"Well, Nox is what he went by when I had the 'pleasure' of knowing him. Don't worry, that bastard is dead too," Dean informed her.

"Another dangerous one, but the damage he has caused between his coming here and his passing is probably quite great. He was a man much like this Damian, just as arrogant, and just as consumed by his hunger for power. What made him dangerous was that he could see further than many men who want power. Men like that act with purpose, long reaching purpose. I wonder what ruin he's still bringing, even after death."

Dean huffed. "Well, if you had maybe let us talk before this, we would have told you that that's why we're here. We're not here to repeat Nox's actions. We're here to try to fix the damage that he's caused. Or at least that's what we're hoping to do. But no, you had to attack us and take us prisoner first."

"You didn't strike me as the type to lose his cool so easily."

"Recent events have made me a little testy, so I think that's understandable."

She turned, evaluating him. "Perhaps. Or perhaps it's simply the jungle getting to you. I hear that the heat can affect those that aren't used to it. Make them...more aggressive."

There was a subtlety to her voice that he didn't like and he frowned at her in question. It echoed Katarina's comment about how anxious he had been from the moment they had entered the jungle. His friends all knew that it was possible for him to be affected by the environment he was in, but then again, they knew what he was. This woman didn't, or at least he didn't think she did, but he didn't like that she seemed to be nearing the truth. He didn't know how she was getting so close to it, but he had to check himself before he gave too much away, before he was ready.

"I apologize. It's been a rough few days. Well, a rough year really," Dean admitted, hoping he sounded sincere.

The Watcher stepped closer to him, showing no hesitation or caution as she stepped within arm's reach. Dean wasn't foolish enough to try to hurt her, even if he wanted to. He still had to fight the urge to either step away or push her away from him. He didn't like the feeling that she was piercing into his soul and seeing what lay there.

"You have spirit. I will give you that, Dean. My hunters tell me you managed to best two of our own. They find it amusing, but I find myself curious. You are not a Child of the Moon, yet I'm told you fought with the ferocity of one."

Dean shoved away his irritation at her comment about his 'spirit.' It reminded him too much of Damian's comments along those same lines. The familiar hate, tinged with fear, welled up in him and he pushed that aside too. The man was dead, but he was still haunting Dean from the grave. He would deal with that another time, when he wasn't facing down a stranger who hadn't earned the right to see into his innermost thoughts.

"Anyone who hangs around werewolves for long enough is bound to pick some things up," he said, noting the word she had used for werewolves.

She reached up to place her fingers on his scarred shoulder. "Especially one so intricately tied to one of ours. The one called Mikael, yes?"

He blinked, having forgotten that werewolves could sense a mating bond. "Yes. I know you said the others are okay, but..."

She smiled, thankfully removing her hand from him. "Yes, your mate is safe. He's been quite difficult, that one. Refuses to calm himself until he knows whether you are safe or not. We have been forced to use weapons made of Luna's gift to keep him at bay when we bring him food."

Dean squinted down at her. "Luna's gift? Wait, do you mean silver?"

"Do not worry, we have caused him no permanent harm. We only used enough to make him retreat from his persistent attacks. The metal is quite painful to our kind, as you know. Painful enough to make even the staunchest of warriors rethink their decision to attack. I will give him credit. Despite knowing we have them, he continues to try. He must love you very much."

Dean's hands balled into fists at his sides. "He does and I him. And if you've hurt him, I swear, I'll-"

She turned, her look sharp. "You'll what?"

Dean narrowed his eyes. "For him? I would burn this whole jungle down. I promise you that."

"Humans. You're always so sure of yourselves."

There was amusement in her voice and it irked him. "Look, I've learned a lot about what I'm capable of over the past year. Some of it is great and some of it is...things I still need to figure out how I feel about. But I know for a fact that if you hurt Mikael or any of the others, I'm going to find out some other things I'm capable of, and I bet it won't be pretty."

She leaned in closer to him as the woman on guard duty spoke in that strange language of theirs. Dean still couldn't figure out what it was. The Watcher responded softly, still gazing up into Dean's eyes. Dean glared back down at her, meaning every word he said. Everyone who had come with him was his family, and he knew just how important family really was. If he had to do something drastic, dangerous, and ill-advised in order to save them, then he would do it without a thought. Any consequences from that choice could be dealt with afterward.

"Fear not, Dean. I have no intention, at the moment, of causing you or yours harm. Even the other two, when we find them. Let us hope that you never have to come to that decision," she told him softly before stepping away.

"At the moment?" he asked.

"Yes. You are not the only one with a fierce loyalty to

those you care about. I have that, and my duty to protect this place and all that it holds. I have failed in that duty only once and I won't do so again. I do not know if you are a threat or not, or if you truly mean to try to undo whatever damage the fallen one has caused."

Dean glanced at the guard. "So, what? We're going to be your prisoners until you make up your mind?"

"I will talk with the others as I have spoken to you. One or all of you will tell me what I need to know at some point. It is just a matter of time. But yes, you will be kept here until I come to my decision. You cannot be allowed to roam free. Once, those who sought what lay here might have been able to walk more freely, but I have learned my lesson about giving so much trust to outsiders."

"Am I at least allowed to see the others? To let Mikael know I'm okay?" Dean asked, hopeful.

"I will speak to each of you individually, to hear the tale you all tell without interference from the rest. After I have spoken to you all, perhaps then you may see one another again. For now, your separation will continue."

He couldn't say that he blamed her, it made a lot of sense. If she was going to see if their stories lined up, it wouldn't do to have them be able to talk to one another. He had no doubt though, that the others would tell her pretty much the same thing he had. It just bothered him that he wouldn't be able to see them and confirm she wasn't lying to him about them being safe.

"Don't take too long with that," he told her, feeling stubborn again. "Because trust goes both ways. You can check our stories to make sure we're telling the truth, but if you hold me away from them for too long, I'm going to have no choice but believe you've been lying to me."

She laughed at that, turning to walk away. "And what have I done for you to believe that of me?"

"Probably the same thing I did to earn being treated like a criminal."

The Watcher motioned to the younger woman. "You speak fairly. Do not worry, Dean. You and I will speak again and soon I hope. For now, I ask that you return to your cell until I call upon you again."

CHAPTER 16

He would give the Watcher credit: the woman didn't bother to mince words when she didn't have to. The room they were keeping him in really did count as a cell. The people who brought him food were no more responsive than they had been before and the door let no more light in. He thought it was a bit unfair, since even criminals back home were at least allowed a book and some recreation time between periods being locked up.

Instead, he was left with an almost completely dark room and his own thoughts. He had tried to connect with the jungle like he had when he'd been locked up in the mountain. But even though he was not directly in the jungle the overpowering sensation of the energies was not alleviated. It wasn't quite as bad as the first time he'd attempted it, but it was still overwhelming to feel it pounding through him.

With all the time he had when he was left to his own devices, he was given the opportunity to make more than one attempt at it. Each one was met with failure, no matter how cautious he was about reaching out. Each time was met with the greedy pulse of life that had filled him right from his first attempt. Even the slightest sliver of awareness had him almost immediately backing up and shutting it down before it overtook his ability to handle it. The only real success he could claim was that it wasn't giving him a pounding headache anymore.

When the door opened and the woman who had served as a guard for his talk with the Watcher walked in, he knew it was time. The wait had been longer this time, but it hadn't been nearly as long as he feared it would be. Another few days, maybe? He wasn't really sure. He only knew he'd been in here longer than he wanted to be. He had expected to have to wait, since it sounded as if they hadn't found Apollo or Dante when he had been dragged before her.

"You know, I could really use a shower. Or a bath, a really long bath," he told his escort, who only motioned for him to follow.

He followed as she led him through the same halls as she had the first time he'd been brought before the Watcher. This time, however, they didn't stop at the lush courtyard, but took one of the paths that circled around the center pool. There was another set of stairs at the back that took them up into a large room. The high walls had tall openings cut into them, set at the northern and southern ends, allowing light, but not direct sunlight, into the room.

There were small tables with cushions spread out before them. At the back of the room was another small set of stairs. At the top was a large stone bench with a solid back to it, and a plush cushion on the seat. There were many of the tribal people in there, laid out comfortably on cushions as they ate, talked quietly, or simply rested. The

Watcher sat on the large cushion on the raised bench, staring down the length of the room.

The conversations in the room petered out when Dean and his escort walked in. No one in the room bothered to hide their interest at the sight of him. It was then that he saw there was a collection of tribe members off to the side of the Watcher's stone bench. They stood, silver tipped weapons in hand, over another table surrounded by cushions. He knew his face lit up as they approached, when he spotted the familiar faces sat there.

Silun immediately beamed when he saw Dean approaching, raising a hand to wave vigorously at him. Relief flooded Katarina's face when she saw where Silun was waving. Mikael's face was difficult to read, but Dean could see the conflict of emotions there. He was certainly relieved, frustrated, and from the glare he shot the Watcher, pissed. Dean smiled softly at him, shrugging a little because after all, what could they do?

"Decided we didn't have to be locked up for everyone's safety, huh?" Dean asked as they reached the bottom of the stairs leading to the bench.

"I did say that I wished to talk to everyone in your group before I proceeded," she told him, seemingly unfazed by his attitude.

One glance at the table told him that she hadn't spoken to everyone. If that were true, he would see Apollo and Dante there. Their absence told him they still hadn't found the two men and Dean found that curious. No matter how skilled they might have been when left to their own devices, they were at a disadvantage. The people here knew the land as well as Apollo and Dante would know the lands around the Grove. How they were managing to keep under the radar and not get caught was interesting.

"Got our stories all checked out?" Dean asked, avoiding the subject of the missing two for the moment.

"More or less," the Watcher replied, her gaze flicking to Katarina for a moment before returning to Dean.

Dean raised a brow in question at Katarina who shrugged. "I wasn't telling her anything. I told her to eat shit."

Beside her, Silun winced, but Dean laughed. Even Mikael looked amused for a moment as he continued to stare at Dean. It was exactly the sort of answer Dean would have expected Katarina give. It was probably right along the lines of what Dante would have said too, if they had caught him.

"Spirited bunch," the Watcher noted, sounding almost amused.

"Some more than others," Silun commented wryly from where he sat, still wincing but now it was aimed at the Watcher.

"Hey, I thought Children of the Moon are supposed to be spirited?" Dean asked, knowing he was being cheeky.

"We are," the Watcher replied. "Though that doesn't quite explain you, now does it? Unless of course, you are something more than human. Would you happen to know anything about that, Child of the Sun?"

Dean's pulse quickened as several thoughts raced through his mind. The first was that either she had known all along or one of the others had told her when she questioned them. The pained expression on Silun's face immediately told him that the latter was more likely. Dean felt he should have been annoyed, but he couldn't blame the teenager. Silun wouldn't have known just how important that information was or how dangerous it could have been. That, and from the look of him at that table, he was still somewhat lost in all the spiritual energy that was probably around them.

The next thought that hit him was that was twice this woman had used an ancient term that Dean only knew from the myths he had read about and learned. It was quite possible she knew more about those stories than he already knew and that she would be able to tell him more. And their journey here to learn about the crystals might not have been a total waste of time after all.

His excitement must have shown on his face, because the Watcher smiled. "I will take that as a yes, then."

It was already out in the open, so Dean nodded. "You would be correct."

"Interesting, since your kind is supposed to be gone from this world. Before we address that however, I must ask, why keep that from me?"

Dean shrugged. "Two reasons. First, like I said, you haven't exactly done anything to make me want to trust you. I still don't trust you, but you already know about me so there's no point in trying to hide it anymore. Second, people knowing what I am tends to attract a lot of trouble. Hell, it attracted trouble to me before I even knew what I was. Nox wanted me so badly just because he sensed something was different about me, but he didn't actually know what it was. Only good thing that came from dealing with him is that he's the reason I was able to figure out properly what I am."

She nodded at that. "Power draws power, sometimes before we're ready to handle it. I imagine being the first of your kind to appear in generations does attract its fair share of trouble."

"First?" Dean asked.

"Oh yes. Where one Child of the Sun appears, others are sure to follow. Both Children have had their own share of the lost, those of the Sun more so. More and more Children of the Sun were lost, ignorant of what they were or what they could do. Until there were no more to continue on the traditions of their predecessors. There are many more like you out in the world, Dean: humans who are unaware of the gift they possess. But now that one has awakened? I suspect a great deal more will begin to awaken. These sorts of things have a way of building on themselves."

Dean stared in shock. "There...might be more?"

She nodded. "I can't say for sure, but yes, I believe so. And you will be the only Child of the Sun with the knowledge to guide them."

Dean sputtered, "Me? I don't know hardly anything about what it means to be a druid! I've been dealing with this for months and I've barely learned anything."

"If what you have said is true, then you have been through quite a bit in the past year, yes? I bet you have learned more than you believe you have."

"What, that being a druid is going to bring me a whole heap of trouble?"

She chuckled. "Being the firstborn is always challenging. All the responsibility you have for those who will come after."

"And I thought being an only child was scary," Dean muttered, lightheaded at the thought that other druids might "awaken" in the world.

"I must admit to being a little curious, as I have never spoken with a Child of the Sun in all my years. How does our home feel to you?"

"Chaos," Dean answered bluntly. "Total chaos. I don't know what's up with this place, but it's so full of energy that I can't talk to it. Everything here is so eager to grow and eat, it almost knocked me on my ass the first time I tried to connect with it. I've tried a couple of times while you had me locked up, but I can't seem to get a hold on it."

She nodded, looking unsurprised. "This place is filled with the energies of life, as you have figured out. Even the spirits here are those of chaos and growth. Those things that are difficult to control and wield."

"Is it because it's a jungle?" Dean asked.

"Oh, I'm sure many other places like this are full of life energy. Ours, however, is unique because of the strength of it."

"But why here?"

She glanced around the room, taking a moment before replying. "We will come to that, just as we will come to the question I know you have over what the fallen one found when he came here."

"So, you will answer my questions about the crystals?"

There was a twitch at the corner of one of her eyes. "Perhaps. Tell me, what do you know of the Destroyer? Or perhaps you have heard the version that speaks of it as a great darkness?"

"That it once almost destroyed the world and that it took the combined efforts of both Children in order to stop it."

She nodded. "That is the tale most commonly told."

Dean raised a brow. "But I'm guessing that it's not the most accurate version of events?"

"That all depends on how you choose to see it."

Dean frowned. "Now you're just being cryptic."

She laughed. "When you are dealing with old tales that go back further than most civilizations, being cryptic is just part of it."

She had him there. "So what's your version?"

"That long ago, all that existed, existed in pure

harmony. There were three almighty beings who shaped the cosmos and all that lay within it. There were different names and titles for each. The first was the formless one, who made all things, without intention or purpose. You would know him as Creation, the force of life. The second was the static one, who shaped all things, gave them intention and purpose. You would know her as Order. The last was the destructive one, who destroyed all things, who broke them down and returned them to the cycle. You would know him as Entropy. And all three worked in harmony with one another, each doing what the other could not and bringing about the whole of all that we know."

He could see where this was going, even as she explained. Nothing that would come from Creation would last very long. Without the form and function given by Order, nothing would survive long enough to do more than exist for moments at a time. The two of them together would form all the things that could or would ever be. The last, the being of destruction, would break them down, removing the weak, and looping the base materials back around to be reused by Creation. It had the synergy of perfect balance that he had seen in other creation myths in the past and it was familiar to him.

"But that harmony didn't last, did it?" Dean asked, thinking of the version he knew, where a darkness tried to destroy everything.

She shook her head. "No, it did not. No one is quite sure why, though there are plenty who would offer up their own ideas. Whatever the reason, Entropy, the Destroyer went mad. Or whatever you would call it when beings beyond our reckoning extend beyond their given limits. Whatever the case, in his madness, he sought to devour the world, the entire cosmos as a whole. His hunger was without limit, and he deemed the entirety of all to be worth destroying."

"Just curious, what are some of the theories of why that happened?" Dean asked.

"Some say that the Destroyer simply sought more power. Others say that he grew tired of cleaning up after the other two. Then there are those who say that Order and Creation did too much, and drove the Destroyer to the madness that made him wish to devour everything. It matters little, as in the end, it was his goal that was important."

Which meant doing his job a little too well. Something had happened to throw everything out of balance and this force of entropy and destruction went overboard. Dean could see how a force that was meant to be a balancer through destruction could be referred to as the Darkness if looked at in a certain way.

She watched him for a moment before continuing. "In his madness, his power became corrupted. No longer did he balance the scales, but instead sought to tip them into his maw. Corruption spread, infecting the world like a disease. Nothing was safe from the corrosive effect of the Destroyer. After all, corrupted entropy is still entropy, but it is greedy and without restraint. It can also be a fount of great power for those willing to serve and the Destroyer found many a servant in others."

"People like Nox? The ones who you call fallen?"

Her face was grim as she nodded. "The effects of the Destroyer are insidious and far-reaching. There are those, like this Nox, who fell willingly. Whether out of greed for power or simple zealotry to bring about the end, they choose their corruption. Far less despicable were those who were slowly corrupted, whether through excessive exposure to the corrupted energies of the Destroyer or through a weakness of character. They were servants all the same, but servants who were tricked rather than having chosen their path."

From the look on Silun's face, Dean could see the younger man was thinking about the shamans in the mountain as well. "Was there...any cure for it?"

"The corruption? The only cure that has ever been spoken of was death. That is far kinder than letting them continue in the wretched state that I'm sure they existed in."

She paused, staring down at him for a moment before glancing at the table beside her. Silun avoided her gaze, while Mikael never bothered to look at her at all. He was looking at Dean with a look of sad understanding, having apparently come to the same train of thought that Dean was on. It should have relieved Dean that he had made the right choice by letting the shamans die, but it didn't. While it seemed true that there had been no way to save them from their fate, he wished he had gotten there sooner and perhaps been able to at least save his friend before it had come to that.

"You have seen what I speak of, haven't you?" she asked finally.

Dean took a deep breath and nodded. "A...friend of ours."

He glanced at Mikael, wondering if he should tell the story or not. His instincts told him to tell this woman, but he had promised to stop excluding Mikael from his decisions. His mate hesitated a moment before nodding, giving a little shrug. Dean read into the shrug the same thing that he was thinking: *what would it hurt to tell them?*

So, he told her the story, starting with the tale of when

Damian and Nox first came to the Grove. Of the war that had come out of it after Damian's failed coup and Nox's death at him and Mikael's hands. Of the tube they had found on Lucille, and how it eventually led to the kidnapping of the shamans. He was careful to skirt around some details, especially when he reached the point of the story where they had invaded the mountain, seeking to free the shamans.

The Watcher barely spoke throughout the telling of the story, only nodding or asking a brief question for the sake of clarity. When he finished, she sat on her bench in silent thought. Dean felt exhausted after having told the whole story, feeling somewhat amazed that it hadn't taken long to tell. It had been months of his life, sometimes filled with days of hell and pain, but it had barely taken him half an hour to tell all of it.

"That," she began finally, looking up at him. "Is almost precisely what the old tales told of when they spoke of the corruption of the Destroyer gone mad. I cannot describe the anger and worry I feel to know that my failure to fulfill my duty led to all of that. I am sorry, Dean. Were it not for my failings, you would not have had to endure all of that. My weakness led to this."

Dean's surprise couldn't have been any more obvious. He had been expecting information and hopefully a slow build of trust between himself and the Watcher. The idea that she might apologize to him for Nox had never entered his mind. The undiluted regret in her voice stopped the next words out of his mouth in their tracks.

In some way, he wanted to place all of the blame on this woman. He had known something was wrong with Nox early on in his dealings with the fallen shaman. It would be so easy to place the fault in the hands of this woman who had failed in the duty she had tried to uphold for most of her life.

It was too easy to blame her though and he knew that. He didn't see it as any different to his failure to intercept and prevent Damian's actions before they happened. Were it not for his own failings and those of others, perhaps Damian and Nox wouldn't have been able to cause the damage they did. At the very least, if he had been quicker to gain an understanding, he might have been able to save the shamans from the hell they had been dragged into before it was too late.

He shook his head. "There's no need to apologize to me or to any of us. We could blame each other or ourselves until the sun stopped burning, but it wouldn't change what happened. What's done is done, and now we have to try to clean up the mess that a couple of arrogant, power-hungry assholes have left behind for us."

The woman who had served as his escort glanced at him, then at the Watcher. "I like him."

Dean glanced at her in surprise. "You speak English, too?"

She smirked at him. "Of course, I am the Learner. Or at least, that's what I would be in your tongue."

Dean glared at the two women. "And how many others around here are able to clearly understand us?"

The Learner laughed. "Only a few and they only speak a little. One day, I will take my grandmother's place as the Watcher. For now though, I am to learn and grow so that I am fit to take her position when the time comes."

He glanced between the two women, trying to separate the years between them in his mind. If he replaced the silver of the Watcher's hair with dark brown, reduced the lines on her face, and made her eyes darker, he could see it.

It wasn't a strong family resemblance, but now that he knew it was there, he could see it more clearly. It was close to the similarities between Mikael and his mother, but one had to know what to look for.

"Uh," he began, remembering his first interaction with her. "Just so you know, that first day, I wasn't trying to stare at you because I was interested or anything."

That made both women laugh and Mikael shot him a curious look. Dean felt the heat rise on his face under the scrutiny of his mate and he shrugged weakly. Considering he hadn't thought he would be able to explain himself to her that first day, he hadn't thought it important to point out that fact. Now that he knew she spoke English as well as her grandmother, he didn't want that little misunderstanding to hang in the air.

"Don't worry yourself, Dean. I have been outside of this jungle in my lifetime, as all Learners before me have. I know the custom of covering the female chest, but it serves no purpose here, no practical one anyway. I laughed that day because you looked so startled by it, I could not help it. And it soon became apparent that you were well spoken for, by the handsome Child of the Moon who, incidentally, hasn't stopped watching you since we entered," the Learner said, with a flick of her hand toward Mikael.

It was Mikael's turn to blush, though Dean knew it was more at being called handsome by this strange woman than for being caught staring at Dean. Other than failing to stand up to Samuel in the beginning, Mikael had never shrunk away from being openly affectionate with Dean, or protective. It amused Dean to think that Mikael was slated to be the future Alpha of his pack and that he was confident and assured, more than most people he had ever met. Yet, all it took was a pretty face calling him attractive and he turned bright red and averted his gaze.

Deciding to move the conversation along, Dean turned back to the Watcher. "I'm glad you all approve of my mate and aren't going to string me up for being a Druid. But you are telling me all of this for a reason, what is it?"

The Watcher leveled her gaze with his, the lines on her forehead etching deeper. He hadn't realized it when he'd asked the question, but he had just pushed their interaction to the next stage. If he was guessing correctly, she was considering whether or not he was worthy of the trust he suspected she wanted to give him. She had to weigh what she knew about them against her experience of outsiders in the past.

The Learner shifted anxiously beside him and began to speak to her grandmother in their language. The Watcher's eyes never left Dean's, but the frown on her face deepened. When the Learner finished speaking, the Watcher closed her eyes and took a deep breath. When her mismatched eyes opened once more to rest on Dean's, he could see the wary acceptance behind them.

"My granddaughter speaks wisely, if not a little impatiently. She is correct in the fact that you have shown no signs of violence or trickery. What you concealed from me was warranted due to your own experience, but you chose to divulge it openly once I approached you on it civilly. You have shown a remarkable mixture of spirit and wisdom, something that one of your years does not normally have. My duty is to the safety of this world, not just to my people. She may indeed be correct in that I may have failed in that duty by allowing this Nox the trust I gave him, but I may also risk failing in that duty by not giving you the same trust."

The Learner nodded once sharply and Dean glanced between them. "What does that mean?"

The Watcher stood up and motioned for him to approach. "It means you must come with me. There is something I must show you and much I still have to tell."

CHAPTER 17

S he led him down into the darkness of the large structure that served as her tribe's home. It was just him and the Watcher; her guiding him down the twisting staircases that led into the bowels of the building. It grew darker and cooler as they descended, far enough down that he was sure that they had gone below ground level. The air still had the smell of dry dust to it, but somewhere in the distance he could smell something damp and unpleasant that he couldn't quite place.

Thinking of the many hallways he had seen leading off the stairway, he glanced at the Watcher. "What were those other hallways? The ones we passed on the way down here?"

She never looked at him, keeping her gaze on the path ahead. "Other places where we keep various objects. Some of them are kept down here where they can be preserved, for the sake of our own personal tales. Others are objects too dangerous to be left out in the open, but we cannot yet destroy them ourselves. This place has always been one that has housed and protected the knowledge of the eons. Sometimes that protection is for the sake of the world, rather than the objects themselves."

Dean thought about that for a moment before replying. "And what are you going to show me? Are you protecting it from the world or the world from it?"

The air at the bottom of the stairs was stale and held the unpleasant smell he had detected on the way down. The stairs opened up into a square room, lit by torches. There wasn't a part of the room that wasn't illuminated by the flames of those torches. They were so numerous and bright, that the only shadows cast now were by their bodies.

"None are permitted down here save for me or those that I bring down here to replace the seals," she explained as she approached the wall to the left of where they had entered.

"Seals?" Dean asked, feeling a growing sense of foreboding in the back of his mind as he followed her to the wall.

"It sounds strange to you, who has only taken his first, albeit large, steps into a world beyond the human one. But yes, seals. The dangerous items we house here are all kept sealed, so they are safe from being found or from influencing the world around them in some way. What lies down here must be kept under the most intricate and potent seals we have and they must be renewed every decade or so. The knowledge of these seals are the last step to becoming a Watcher."

He stopped, frowning at her. "That seems like really important knowledge to have, in case something should happen to you. What exactly do these seals do that they would be treated as though they were dangerous knowledge?"

She stopped before the wall, turning to him, her eyes

glittering in the torchlight. "You remain as astute as ever, Dean. The seals manipulate the energy of whatever is kept within them. One set is designed to pull the energy out, drawing it into the next set of seals which weaken and dilute the energies they draw upon. The last set is made to release the energy out into the world safely, a bit at a time, where the energy is too weak, particularly here in this land, to do much more than dissipate."

Dean's mind ran over that and a chilling thought occurred to him. "Someone who knows these seals and how they work...They would be able to change how they work, wouldn't they? To enhance the power of whatever is locked behind them or to harness it."

She nodded grimly. "Knowledge is a dangerous and oftentimes double-edged blade Dean. Never forget that."

The image of the journal rose up in his mind and he groaned. "And let me guess, you brought Nox down here, didn't you?"

The Watcher turned back to the wall, drawing a dagger from her belt and pricking her index finger. "Yes. It was not for long, but it was long enough for the damage to be done. He got his hands on that which was not meant for him, which included the knowledge of some of the seals. The journal you had with you contained some of the symbols that work as our seals, though thankfully not all of them."

"But enough that someone might be able to do something with them," Dean added grimly as he watched her trace the bloodied finger over the wall. At first nothing happened, until he heard a dull clunk from somewhere deep in the wall. Cracks appeared, straight lines that formed the rectangular shape of a door. It opened, with the push of her bloodied hand, into another hallway that was again lit with torches everywhere. It ended in a solid wall.

"Who keeps these torches going?" Dean asked, wondering how they could have kept going in the sealed tunnel.

"Spirits of fire are attracted to the high energies of this place, seeking sustenance. With enough skill and knowledge, a shaman can convince them to do a great many things. Keeping a fire going for longer than it should be physically able to is one such trick," she told him, waving her fingers at the torches as they passed.

He had expected to walk to the end of the hallway, where the same trick would be repeated to open another door. Instead, she stopped three-quarters of the way down and faced the wall on the left. She tapped the wall and handed the small blade over to him. Dean took it automatically before hesitating, realizing what it was that she wanted.

"Will your blood not work again?" he asked, eyeing his own fingers.

"The spirits we have harnessed to the mechanisms of these walls and doors will not accept the same sacrifice of life energy twice. At least not in such rapid succession. There must always be two to open these doors and always the sacrifice of life force must be done willingly, or the spirits will not respond."

Dean turned the blade over, letting the edge shine in the torchlight. "And why is that?"

She smiled up at him. "Because the spirits housed here are old, older than any living civilization in the world. They come from a time when respect and adherence to the established laws of existence were heeded by their kind. They are...traditionalists, very staunch. They would see the act of an unwilling sacrifice as an insult, akin to pissing on the graves of your family."

"Well there's a lovely image," Dean wrinkled his nose, thinking about his parents' and grandfather's graves.

She reached out and stopped him before he pressed the sharpened tip to the ball of his finger. "A moment, please. What lies beyond this doorway is the most dangerous object in existence, that I know of. To even be in the same room will be a great danger to you. The more adept to the whole of the world, as you as a druid, or I as a shaman are, the greater the danger. Think carefully about this decision. I will think no less of you if you should choose to turn away now."

Dean could see she was as serious as she had been when she had spoken her apology to him in what he thought of as her throne room. There was fear behind her eyes that hadn't been there before. He had a suspicion of what lay behind this secret door, and he wanted to tell her it would be alright. He had faced many dark things in the past year, after all.

Still, he could hear his own internal voice chiding him for trying to be impulsive. That impulsivity had almost brought him ruin a few times in the past year, and that habit had grown even worse since coming to the jungle. The voice of caution in his mind worried about what could possibly be on the other side of the door, and if he was ready to find out. He knew what was at stake, both if he stayed on this side of the door and if he were to pass through. Everything he had worked toward could well be on an edge as dangerous and thin as the dagger he held.

He took a deep breath and jabbed the point of the blade into the end of his finger. "I would think less of me, though. Nothing was ever changed in this world by ignoring something just because it could be dangerous, right?"

She said nothing, watching his face carefully as he

mirrored her actions from before, smearing the bloodied finger along the point she indicated. There was another pause, then the familiar sound resonated from deep within the wall. It was already a fascinating mechanism, but for him to know that it was spirits that ran the device that operated it made it all the more fascinating to him.

The lines had only just formed on the door when he felt a rush of lightheadedness pass through him. He could feel the Watcher's hand on his arm stiffen as something icy cold seeped into him. It had nothing to do with the temperature of the air. It was skipping and touching his skin and his bones and moving straight into the very core of his being.

"Hell," he muttered as he reached out to hold himself steady against the wall. Through his swimming sight, he could see a familiar blue light pulsing out from around the edges of the door that had now formed. Through the tangle of his thoughts, he knew that his suspicion had been right. He knew what lay beyond this door.

The coldness was so much more than just a sensation and it took him a moment to come to terms with it shifting through his mind. Yes, it was the death and horror it had been when he walked into the room, in the bowels of the mountain that Damian had made into his own private fortress. It was everything cold and dark in the world, bubbling up from the bottom of his mind and bringing with it all the awful things that lay there.

He reeled under the onslaught of his mind as the energy seeping from the room found his every personal tragedy. The horror of his parents' and his grandfather's deaths. The aching loneliness of his years after the loss of every family member he had. The despair at the monotony his life had become: safe and secure, but lacking any real purpose or hope. The pain of heartbreak when lovers and friends turned from him, some out of malice, others out of painful ignorance. The same pain that had been so much stronger when he thought he might lose Mikael and the struggle that their lives together had become. The darkness of the cave where he had been tortured, the loss of Artemis, and the pain of having to leave Talon to die under the mountain.

Distantly, he felt the Watcher pull on his arm and say his name. Pulling his arm free from her grip felt like pulling it through thick mud as he tried to get his thoughts in order once more. He was drowning in the despair and agony of whatever was in that room and he didn't know how to pull himself up for air. The energy of the room was supposed to be held in check and muted, but it was finding every weak point within his mind and dragging him down.

"Wait," he gasped, feeling her start to pull him away from the partially open door.

Desperately, he reached his mind out, setting free the last of his defenses against the oppressive darkness. Just as the icy blackness began to take over, he found the thread of power he had been looking for. Even as far underground as they were, he could sense it there and it eagerly dove for the spark of life in his body.

Shudders wracked his body as fire and ice fought within him, colliding in a crash of opposing power. The frantic energy of life and desire slammed against the chilling forces of death and despair. The dark feeling in him was restrained by the seals somewhere in the room. The power of the jungle was diminished by the distance between it and him. The forces were powerful, but they were equal, neither giving an inch for the other. He felt like he was being ripped apart from within, the powers pulling and pushing at him fiercely.

"Like hell," he swore through gritted teeth, finding some

semblance of his mind in the chaos that filled him. That bit of awareness was all he needed and he threw himself before the pulsating energies of the jungle. That was all it took. Like a forest fire, the power burned through him, searing away the icy tendrils wrapping themselves around his soul. He took a gulp of air that sounded too loud to his ears as he burned the dark power out of his entire being, aiding the thriving force of life and creation within him.

With sheer strength of willpower, he closed the floodgates he had opened to the jungle above them. The potency of the jungle's energies began to dissipate, cut in half at first until it became manageable. He didn't know how long he stood there, finding the right balance between the power of the jungle, that allowed him to fight the power of darkness from within the room, while still maintaining a hold on his sense of self. He had come so close to losing himself, and the whole experience left him shaking against the warm stone of the nearby wall.

"Dean?" the Watcher's soft voice, laced with concern, asked from somewhere beside him.

He opened his eyes, seeing her and the barely opened door before him. The familiar, insidious, unnatural blue light that he knew so well pulsed around the edges of the door. Dean could feel the power that lay on the other side, still trying to find a way into his soul. His body was vibrating with the amount of power from the jungle he was allowing into himself, but it was the only safeguard he had against the strength of the crushing darkness mere feet away from him.

"I'm okay, I think," Dean tried to reassure her, unsurprised to hear a quiver in his voice.

"I did not know if you would be as sensitive to the effects of it as a shaman would be. I'm so sorry to have exposed you without any protection," she whispered to him, reaching out to lay her fingers on his arm once more.

He closed his eyes against the warmth of her fingers. "I thought...I thought I would be okay, since I've dealt with it before. There's one of those crystal clusters in there, isn't there? Way bigger than the one I found in Damian's mountain hideout?"

"Yes. You must see it with your own eyes and then I can explain better. You seem to have regained your strength, but are you fit to continue?"

He didn't want to be; that was the first thought to enter his mind. The oppressive bleakness that had pushed against him had been overwhelming. The only saving grace was that he had been able to rely on the source of power that he previously hadn't even been able to brush against without it causing pain. Entering the room meant utilizing a carefully measured amount of a power he barely had control of, hoping that the icy blackness on the other side of that door could be held at bay and that he could also hold the frenetic energies wrapped around him at bay.

"I am," he said truthfully, pushing away from the wall and shaking himself off.

She eyed him carefully before nodding and walking forward to push the door open completely. The dark power of the blue light grew in intensity, pressing against his skin like a blanket of ice. It only took a moment to draw in more power from the jungle, frantically finding the right balance as he tried to follow her. There was a war going on inside of him, one of conflicting desires that weren't completely his own. As they entered the room, he struggled to wrap his mind around it, while keeping his focus on the balance of power.

"Dear God," he gasped as he stepped fully into the room.

The crystal Damian had grown in the depths of his natural fortress was tiny in comparison to the crystal formation before him. It was held by silver bands around its body, suspended over a pit and illuminated by the sickly blue light it emitted. The part he could see was almost three stories high and as wide as a tank. He stepped forward to see that it extended even further into the hole, the sheer size of it enough to crush the average house.

His gaze followed the silver bands wrapped around it and along the chains to the posts the chains were embedded in. Each item had symbols carved into it, the chain having alternating symbols etched into each of its massive links. On the floor, circling the outside of the pillars, were more symbols, different to the others and etched into the stone itself.

The power he had felt on the other side of the door was nothing compared to the power he was feeling now as he stood before the massive crystal. It took another large influx of power from the jungle above to try and balance it out enough for him to think straight. For a moment, he felt the living energies he was drawing on falter before the sheer strength of the crystal. It was only when he stepped further away from the circle of sigils on the floor that he was able to draw sufficient power to keep himself whole.

"It's so big. Holy hell, why haven't you destroyed it?" Dean asked, wincing as he adjusted the internal balance of energies in him once more.

"Once they have grown to a certain size, it is impossible to destroy them. At least, impossible by any means that we possess. I wouldn't even know how to begin to destroy it if we tried, and we *have* tried. Silver weapons work on the newest growth, where the crystal is the most fragile, but they do nothing once you go deep enough beneath the newly formed brittle shell," she told him as she stared at the crystal with an impassive expression.

"Is this...where Nox got his crystals?" Dean asked.

She nodded. "Yes. We stood as you and I are stood now, and when I was preoccupied checking the seals as I do, he took a piece of the crystal nearest him. Once he took the crystal out of this room, however, it was inevitable he would be found out. That man had a wily sense of self-preservation, and was gone before we could take possession of him. I thought that I had found another, from the outside world, who would understand what it was that we have here, and the burden we carry. Little did I know, it was too late, and he understood all too well."

"What...what is it?"

"It's old, very old. It's been here far longer than I can accurately tell. Even the stories of what it was before it came here contradict one another. One tale speaks of it being a weapon against the Destroyer's power. Meant to soak up the effects of its corruption, and contain it so that it could not harm the world. That it was a fool's errand, and the power within the crystal was inevitably corrupted itself, and began to aid the growth of the Destroyer's power. Others speak of how the crystal was a weapon used by the Destroyer's forces, as a source of power for its loyal followers."

Dean stared up at the crystal, thinking it could be beautiful if it didn't feel so twisted. "Guess it doesn't really matter what it was, only what it is."

She nodded. "It feeds upon the energies of death and decay, twisting them to create the corrupting power that the mad Destroyer utilized once, before it was quieted. It is why it is so far down, here in our home, in the center of our land. Between the seals we have put on it and the power of the jungle above, it is contained...mostly. It still grows, little by little, yet it still grows nonetheless. We cannot stop it from growing, but we have been able to slow it down considerably. Now its growth is measured in spans of centuries, rather than the mere weeks that an uncontained crystal would take."

"Like the ones Damian had."

"Such as the pieces that this Damian had. He lacked the knowledge and power to grow them efficiently, but they would grow all the same. Any piece freed from the main body will begin its own crystal formation, feeding off the forces of entropy that will inevitably show up around it. That piece will grow in size, and be able to draw more power from further away. If this Damian had the proper knowledge, he could have used the spiritual power of the stolen shaman to much greater effect than he did. I am glad that he lacked the right knowledge, for any crystal fueled by the strength of several shaman would have been a catastrophe. His ignorance saved us."

Dean frowned, trying to think back to the size of the crystal Damian had, compared to the one before him. It sounded as if she didn't quite know how long this one had been in existence. It had obviously been around for long enough that it was now essentially indestructible. She had said it was still growing, though very slowly. That would give them time, plenty of time by the sounds of it, but she wouldn't be showing him this if it meant it was just a problem that wouldn't need to be faced for centuries upon centuries.

"Why show me this?" he asked plainly, wishing they

didn't have to talk about this while in the same room as the crystal.

She turned to him, looking exhausted. "You wanted to know where the pieces came from that Nox had in his possession. Well, here is your answer. This is the proverbial mother from which those pieces were spawned. Four pieces are destroyed, one is safely within your grasp, and the other is still unaccounted for. You also now know precisely what is at stake. You have also felt the strength of a formation that is being actively held in check in every way that we know how. You know what could happen if one of those pieces fell into knowledgeable hands and were allowed to grow unchecked."

Dean didn't want to think about that, not here. The idea of one of those crystals being allowed to grow strong enough to become immune to destruction was too much for him to ponder. Not here, where the power of the crystal was still bearing down on his mind, still trying to swallow him whole.

"Now what?" he asked, feeling his legs beginning to shake as he still fought to keep himself internally balanced.

"Now we leave this place and then you are to rest. I hadn't known how this place would affect you. No shaman, without years of proper training, is permitted to come this far, not even to the bottom of the stairs. It seems that your kind are just as sensitive, though in a totally different way. It has taken its toll on you and I hope you are strong enough to resist any of its lingering effects."

"Watcher," he gasped, stumbling back toward the doorway. "I'm going to pass out. I would really like to do that as far away from this room as possible."

She had no time to react before he turned and rushed out of the room as quickly as his wobbly legs would carry him. The powerful energies working within him were sapping his strength rapidly. The exhaustion he was feeling was making the strength of the crystal's energy grow. As his strength ebbed, the power of the jungle weakened as well. He was struggling to maintain the precarious balance.

His vision spun and he could just make out the bottom of the stairs. He stumbled against the wall, feeling his stomach contents bubble up and out of his mouth. His stomach muscles heaved, aching as he emptied his guts onto the stone floor. He gasped for air, fighting against the pain, wiping his mouth as he stumbled and fell onto the stairs.

Dean rolled over, his vision going dark at the edges. Though his sight was blurry, he could see the Watcher hurriedly closing the outer door, having apparently closed the inner one while he had been puking. Relief flooded him as he realized the icy grip threatening his mind was gone. He wasn't able to hold on to the strength that allowed him to hold back the thriving power of the jungle any longer, and unconsciously, he slammed the door closed.

"Oh good, you got the door," he mumbled as the darkness of his vision overtook him and he slumped into unconsciousness.

CHAPTER 18

He was warm; not the oppressive warmth of the jungle, but the comfortable warmth of being curled up in bed beside Mikael. Dean could feel the muscles of his body working, stretching a little as he took a deep breath. He gave a soft groan of pleasure as the familiar smell of his mate filled his senses, bringing him closer to the surface of consciousness. There was a hard body against his, contrasting marvelously with the softness that lay beneath him.

His mind was alert enough now that he realized he was curled up on some sort of plush bed or cot. The warmth up against him was Mikael's, his arms comfortably holding Dean's body. It was so soothing to lay there against him, taking in the heat and smell of him. Everything about it spoke of the comforts of home and he wished he was there right now, even if his mind tried to insist that that's exactly where he was.

"I know you're awake," Mikael's soft voice said above him.

"Shh, was having nice thoughts," Dean protested, wriggling against Mikael, trying to get even closer to him.

"What sort of thoughts were those?"

Dean cracked an eye, looking up at Mikael and smiling. "I was thinking how laying with you feels like home. Been so miserable about being stuck in this jungle, far from home. Kind of just realized that I've actually had home with me the whole time."

Mikael's expression softened, eyes warm as he bent to kiss Dean. "I love you so much, you know that?"

Dean sighed against the kiss, feeling a warmth that had nothing to do with their body heat blossoming inside of him. "I do. Almost as much as I love you."

Mikael's hand slapped Dean's ass with a sharp sound. "Then why do you keep putting yourself in situations that end up with you being hurt or out cold?"

"Ow! Mikael!" Dean protested, now fully awake and pushing himself upright.

"Well?" Mikael demanded.

"I tell you that you feel like home, we exchange mushy sentiments, and then you slap my ass?"

Mikael narrowed his eyes. "You left with that woman for a couple of hours and come back unconscious. You've been out cold for a couple of days now. These strange people I don't know, keep telling me you're fine."

Dean blinked up at Mikael. "Wait. I've been asleep for a couple of days?"

"Almost three actually. That Watcher woman said you were fighting off some force you hadn't known how to deal with properly because you weren't trained. She told me it was amazing that you were fighting so well with little help from anyone else. Tried to say that it was because you were a Child of the Sun, but I told her it was because you were a hard headed son of a bitch who didn't know how to stay down."

Dean couldn't help but laugh at the righteous anger in Mikael's voice and face. He knew Mikael wasn't really angry with him, only letting off steam from the past few days worth of worry. He leaned forward, kissing Mikael soundly and smiling when he felt the tension in Mikael's body leech away at the touch.

"You gotta stop doing that stuff Dean," Mikael whispered, reaching up to stroke Dean's jaw with his thumb.

"I swear to you, it isn't intentional."

"My mate, the trouble magnet," Mikael said fondly, kissing Dean a little more hungrily than before.

"I know that was meant to be a term of endearment, but it doesn't sound very endearing at the moment," Dean protested.

Mikael's mouth found his jaw, nipping slightly at the warm skin. "Maybe I can make you feel better?"

Dean glanced around the small, simply furnished room they were in. The windows along the walls were dark and there was only one door. They were definitely alone, but he wondered just how far away everyone else was. That, and he knew how well sound could carry along stone.

"Is this a good idea, considering where we are?" Dean asked, wriggling as he felt Mikael's hands grip him.

"None of the others are around and I don't care if the Watcher's people hear anything," Mikael told him as he kissed Dean's neck.

Any protests he might have had died as Mikael's hands slipped lower. Dean hadn't realized he was naked until he felt Mikael's hands slip beneath the cover, cupping his groin. Dean groaned against Mikael's hair, pushing his hips into the grip. It was probably a bad idea to do this right now, but he was beginning to care less and less about that at the moment.

"We don't have our stuff," Dean said faintly.

"So?"

"So we don't have any lube."

Mikael shrugged, nipping gently at Dean's collarbone. "That's what hands and mouths are for, babe."

Any remaining resistance Dean might have had shredded at that single remark. Everyone already knew they were mated and they had been left unsupervised. After everything that had happened in the room with the crystal, Dean craved the desire and warmth of Mikael's touch.

His fingers dove into the strands of Mikael's hair and he rolled his hips against him. He could feel Mikael's hardness against his thigh, slipping further down his leg as Mikael worked his way lower. Mikael worked a steady line of kisses down Dean's body, shoving the thin blanket away. When he reached Dean's groin, he gripped hold of his cock, pecking soft kisses in a circle around it.

Even in tender moments like this, neither of them were very good at patience and Mikael wasted no time in placing his mouth around the head of Dean's cock. Dean groaned as he felt the familiar warmth slip around the sensitive head. His fingers gripped a little tighter in Mikael's hair as he felt himself pushed deeper into his mate's throat.

Bright hazel eyes flashed as Mikael gazed up at him. Dean groaned louder, knowing that Mikael was doing it intentionally. Dean had a weakness for being able to watch someone when they sucked him, especially if they made eye contact. It was even more arousing when it was Mikael and Dean shuddered watching Mikael's eyes slide shut in pleasure as he took Dean deep again.

"Hell babe," Dean muttered, pushing his hips up.

Mikael pulled off his cock long enough to slide up and kiss Dean hungrily. Both of them moaned into the kiss as Mikael's hand wrapped around Dean. Dean had seen Mikael do this before and he knew why he was sliding his fingers along Dean's slick length. Anticipation tingled inside him, he shivered under their shared kiss.

When it broke, Dean locked onto Mikael's lust heavy eyes as Mikael positioned himself at Dean's crotch. One hand wrapped around the base of his cock while his mouth took in the head, sucking deep. Dean lifted his hips, feeling one of Mikael's now prepared fingers pushing against the ring of muscles of his ass. There was a moment of pressure and then Mikael's finger slid in.

Dean didn't know which way he wanted to push his hips. Both the finger within him and the mouth around him were tantalizing and his hips wriggled in indecision. Mikael hummed, a deep throaty noise that drove Dean crazy. It vibrated deep, drawing another wave of pleasure out of him as Mikael's finger curled, brushing along the sensitive nerves inside him. He gasped out Mikael's name, finding his grip on the bed as he pushed up into his mate's mouth.

This was nothing like the hard and fast rutting when they had been in the cave, sheltering during the storm. Mikael was taking his time, drawing out the pleasure for as long as he possibly could. It was a testament to his understanding of Dean's body language that he was drawing it out so well. Dean hadn't had a release in days and his ability to hold off with Mikael was normally weak anyway. Mikael moved slowly, letting Dean's cock slide past his lips and into his throat with a measured, torturous pace.

Dean knew that Mikael could draw this out as long as he wanted. There had been times before where Mikael would intentionally take Dean right to the edge, only to pull away and leave him squirming. Part of him desperately hoped this wasn't going to be one of those times, that their circumstances meant Mikael would end it soon. His lover normally only played a waiting game after Dean had at least one or two orgasms already that day. Dean didn't think he could survive it when he hadn't cum in days.

Finally, Mikael pulled free from him with a small noise. "Babe, I'm sorry, but I need to get off. You're too goddamn hot like this."

Relief flooded Dean as he realized he wouldn't have to wait. Leaning forward he pulled at Mikael's armpits, trying to bring him up to him. They were both in need of release and Dean wasn't going to do this one at a time.

"Come here," Dean grunted, still trying to get Mikael to move.

Mikael raised a brow, but allowed Dean to pull him up after pulling his finger free from Dean's ass. Their lips met the moment that Mikael was close enough. Dean pushed his hand down to wrap around Mikael's length. No matter how many times Dean saw or felt Mikael's cock, it always sent a surge of arousal through him. His thumb brushed along the head, already slick with pre-cum and Mikael shuddered above him.

Mikael positioned himself so that he lay more comfortably next to Dean, their bodies turned toward one another. Mikael returned Dean's grip, wrapping his fingers around his cock and stroking. The both of them groaned and pushed against the other's grip. Need and desire surged through them as they tried to bring the other to release.

Dean had thought that he would be the first to cum, but he felt Mikael's body going taut against him. Mikael's kiss became less rhythmic and predictable, his rising need for release making it stutter. His cock pulsed in Dean's hand

and Mikael groaned audibly into his mouth. Cum poured from him, splashing against Dean's stomach and cock.

He would have sworn loudly if his tongue hadn't been fully occupied. Mikael's cum slickened his cock even more and he reached down to hold onto Mikael's wrist to keep his strokes going. It didn't take long before he was pushing against Mikael, feeling his own orgasm ignite within him. Their mouths broke apart as Dean groaned his mate's name, his mind a blissful blank of pure pleasure.

They laid like that for what felt like forever, their foreheads pressed against one another, heaving for breath. It never seemed to matter if they fucked or found some other way to get off. It was always wonderful. The heat and their momentary exhaustion kept them from cradling one another as was their habit, yet Dean didn't have reason to complain. Just having Mikael close, with that utterly content expression on his face was enough.

"Are you okay?" Mikael finally asked once he had regained his breath.

"I'm always okay after that," Dean chuckled.

"I don't mean that."

Dean paused mid stretch, frowning as he tried to wrap his head around whatever train of thought Mikael was on. He remembered why he had been in this bed in the first place and sighed. He supposed that just as he had craved the intimacy between them to help shed the effects of his experience in the depths of the building, Mikael had needed his own reassurance. Their communication with one another had made progress in leaps and bounds, but they still did their best when they were physical with one another.

The soft tiredness on Mikael's face had been replaced by a tightness that Dean hated seeing there. Despite all of his inner strength and confidence, Mikael sometimes still desperately needed reassurance that everything was okay. Dean loved that about him, that despite all the toughness, there was still a vulnerable part of him always in need of attention. No one else but Dean ever got to see that side of him and Dean treasured those moments.

Dean reached out to cup Mikael's face. "I promise you, I'm okay now."

Mikael watched Dean's face carefully. "Are you just saying that?"

Dean shook his head. "I'm not going to hide something like that from you, not something so serious."

"You kept the truth about Damian to yourself and it ate away at you."

Dean smiled. "True, and that was exceptionally stupid on my part. Sometimes I let my independence get the better of me, and my stubbornness. But I would never keep something like this from you. This is something that has to do with what amounts to my soul. If I thought I had been permanently affected by the crystal, even absorbed a little piece of that corruption, I would say something."

Mikael continued to scrutinize him. "Would...would you even know?"

Dean thought about that, realizing it was a question he should have already been asking himself. Would someone even know they were corrupted in the first place? He'd heard it said that crazy people didn't know they were crazy, so it was quite possible that the very same rule could apply to this situation.

After a moment, he shook his head. "I think I would. Talon and all the other shamans knew they were corrupted."

"True, but they also knew they were being exposed to it

through that crystal Damian had. Although, Nox didn't know he was corrupted."

Dean snorted derisively at the thought of the fallen shaman. "Yeah, and Nox was also insane. Delusions of power and grandeur. I also knew that I was being exposed to the crystal, and I don't feel any different. I mean, I'm tired right now, but it took a lot to fight off the effects of the crystal, so that probably accounts for it."

Mikael still looked worried and Dean sighed. How could he explain that other than a little bit of exhaustion, he felt like his normal self? He knew full well what effect the crystal had on him, yet he felt none of that now. Other than concern that Mikael would obsess over this more than he should, there were none of the dark and oppressive thoughts he'd had while in the crystal's presence.

"Look, it's apparently a spiritual corruption, right?" Dean asked, still stroking his fingers down Mikael's cheek.

"That's what everyone keeps saying."

"And the Watcher has been in here several times to check on me, right?"

Mikael nodded. "She's been in here less today, but she was in here a lot before that."

"Then don't you think she would have noticed if something was wrong with me? I'm guessing that in order for her to rule these people, she would have to be a pretty strong shaman, right? And we already know she's got a lot of knowledge when it comes to this sort of thing, so I'm confident she would know corruption in someone when she saw it."

"Except for Nox."

Dean shook his head. "We don't even know if he *was* corrupted then. He could have just been the greedy asshole he'd probably always been and gotten corrupted afterward."

Mikael shook his head. "I don't know, Dean."

"Babe, you're worrying yourself over this so hard. You have to trust me," Dean soothed, pushing himself closer to Mikael.

"I do trust you!" Mikael protested.

"Then why all this nitpicking over details?"

"Maybe because you're my mate? And you're always finding yourself in these situations that could get you killed or worse? And because I can't seem to do anything to help you when you're in those situations?"

Understanding hit Dean and he smiled softly. "That's what it is."

"What?"

"You're feeling helpless because you think you're not helping."

"I'm not!"

Dean pressed himself the rest of the way into Mikael, still smiling. "You're wrong. You help me a hell of a lot more than you're giving yourself credit for right now. Sometimes you're the only thing that gets me through all the hell that has come into my life. Being here with you right now is what tells me there's nothing wrong with me. That the crystal didn't touch me. It might have been strong, but it didn't twist anything inside of me. Loving you and being loved by you is all I feel right now. No darkness, no twisted or hateful desires, just love. That's how it is, how it's been since we got together, how we are. So long as I have you, that's all I'm going to need to keep trying, to keep fighting."

Mikael softened at his words, allowing Dean to hold him. "That won't save your life from someone's jaws or a bullet."

"And I have you and all the others there to help me until I learn to protect myself better. I have you and a new family now, Mikael. I'm so loved and safe that it feels unreal to me at times."

Mikael bit his lower lip. "They all love you."

"And I love them. Even the grumpy one."

Mikael laughed at that, the sound soothing to Dean's ears. "Dante can be a little grouchy, but he's got your back too."

"Exactly, that's my point. I'm surrounded by people who care about me and who I care about. There's so much of it going on in my life that I don't think too much can really touch me now."

Mikael settled down, feeling more relaxed. "You promise to keep training with Katarina when we get back? I think it would be a good idea with everything that seems to be happening or will happen."

Dean thought about all the future bruises he was going to have and nodded as he laid his head down. "I promise. I was thinking the same thing earlier, and I'm sure she would have a great deal of fun smacking me around some more."

"I don't like watching that, but at least it's better in the long run, right?" Mikael asked sleepily.

"I just think of it as Katarina's version of loving me."

They shared a tired chuckled as they ignored the heat of the room and wrapped themselves up in one another. Dean's last thought before he drifted off to sleep was that he didn't know if Mikael's worries were unfounded or not, but that it didn't matter. If he was corrupted, even a little, then maybe it would be destroyed by all the love in his heart. If it wasn't, then he could at least enjoy what he had for a little while before he had to take care of it the only way they knew how. It didn't seem that dark of a thought to him as consciousness slipped away.There were worse deaths than to die loved and cared for.

CHAPTER 19

When he woke, there was sunlight streaming into the room from one of the open windows. Mikael lay next to him, his bright eyes crinkling at the corners as he pulled Dean closer to him. That same blessed relief of being so close to his mate filled Dean once more and he hummed happily against Mikael's skin.

"Good morning, at least I think it's morning," Mikael told him softly.

"Good morning to you too, sleep well?"

"Next to you? Always," Mikael assured him as he rolled himself on top of Dean and kissed him soundly.

"Holy hell, had he even been awake five minutes before you decided to jumped him?" Dante's disgusted voice asked from somewhere behind Dean.

Dean rolled over enough that he could see the tracker clearly. When he saw it was indeed Dante, with Apollo standing quietly behind him, he pushed himself free from beneath Mikael. Dante's eyes went wide as Dean bounded toward him. Dean threw his arms around Dante, squeezing him into a tight hug.

"Holy shit, I didn't know if you guys were alive or not!" Dean exclaimed as he squeezed even tighter.

"Why do I get the naked hugs?" Dante protested.

"Because you were closest," Apollo offered, reaching forward to pry Dean free of Dante.

Dean went happily, hugging Apollo in response. "Seriously, when did they find you guys?"

Apollo patted Dean's back. "They found us not far from here. We hadn't known we had been driven inside their outer defenses and they apparently hadn't expected it. They seemed surprised to have found us where we were."

"Lucky. We got caught the first day," Dean told him.

"Mikael, please?" Dante whined.

"Babe, here," Mikael reached across Dante holding out Dean's clothes. Dean took them, pulling them on quickly as he took in the sight of the two men. They didn't appear to be all that worn down or thin, which meant they had probably survived comfortably out in the jungle. Then again, Apollo had Dean's guide book the entire time, so that probably helped.

"Yeah," Mikael added dryly. "And they seemed really amused when they dragged them in here, too."

Dean turned to him. "Amused, why?"

Mikael shrugged. "No one would say. They told that Watcher woman, and she and her granddaughter got a kick out of whatever it was. These two aren't talking, so I'm betting it's really embarrassing."

Dean turned to the duo. "Care to share with the class?"

Apollo went silent and Dante snorted at him. "Doesn't matter. They found us and that's all that matters. Assholes took all our shit and dragged us here. We thought we were gonna be tortured or something, only to find out you guys already tattled."

"There have been...extenuating circumstances," Dean explained with a roll of his eyes.

"Is he awake, then?"

Dean glanced past Apollo to see the Learner entering the room. She took in the sight of them, and her eyes lingered on Mikael. It was then that Dean realized Mikael hadn't bothered to put on his own clothes yet. Her eyes lingered a little too long and a little too far south for Dean's comfort.

"Now, that's just a shame," she sighed.

"Yeah, yeah," Dean growled, picking up Mikael's pants from the floor and shoving them at him. He quickly found his shirt and threw that at him too all while glaring at the Learner. The woman didn't seem the least bit concerned, staring back at Dean in amusement.

"Wow, was that jealousy?" Dante asked, sounding surprised.

"Don't make me naked hug you again," Dean threatened.

Dante gave him a sour look and the Learner chuckled. "The Watcher says that when you are ready, she wishes to speak with you in the Main Hall once more."

He glanced over his shoulder at Mikael, who, while still red and trying to put his clothes on, nodded at him. Dean shook his head, but motioned that they were ready to go. It took Mikael a moment to hurry after them, now looking a little more disheveled as he tried to adjust his clothing to make himself a little more presentable. He didn't think it really mattered, since the Learner had seen everything there was to see and had clearly enjoyed it.

When they entered the Main Hall, they found the Watcher waiting patiently for them on her stone bench. Katarina and Silun were sitting at the same table where

Dean had last seen them. Katarina seemed to be in less of a foul mood and Silun had been chatting away merrily with the Watcher. Out of all of them, Silun seemed to have gained more of a measure of contentment in his time here. Dean wondered what the shaman had been up to while he had been taking an extended nap.

"It is good to see you on your feet once more Dean. Has your strength returned to you?" the Watcher asked by way of greeting.

"Well, I don't feel like I'm going to puke and pass out, so there's that," Dean replied amiably, smiling at Mikael as his mate passed by to take his spot at the table.

"That's good to hear. Again, I would like to repeat my apologies for exposing you so casually to the effects that you endured down there. Though I must ask, considering how powerful the effects were on you at first, how were you able to withstand it at all?"

Dean explained about using the power of the jungle and how it had taken every part of his willpower to make it work. It had enabled him to have short-term endurance, but he knew it wasn't too surprising that he hadn't been able to maintain it. The Watcher listened with interest, nodding slowly when he finished.

"That was clever thinking on your part and it seems to have saved your life, and soul," the Watcher mused, fingers stroking the edge of the cushion she sat on.

"More like desperation," he snorted.

"Still, I am glad you were able to remove yourself before you lost consciousness. I hesitate to think what would have happened if you had lost consciousness within range of the crystal."

Dean didn't want to think about it, either. When his mind had been able to fight, it hadn't been much of a fight at all. Without using the power of the jungle consciously to fight it off, he would have lost the fight quickly. Without that measure of focus, he would have probably succumbed to what the crystal wanted. He didn't know what being a fallen shaman was like, but if it was anything remotely like the shaman Nox had been, he didn't want to know.

"In that room, you spoke of how the Destroyer had once been quieted, rather than stopped," he began, hoping she would continue the thread.

She nodded. "Of course. No mortal being could ever hope to withstand the full-force of one of those ancient beings, let alone destroy it. And even if one could destroy them, would that be wise? Mad as the Destroyer was, it still had a purpose and without that purpose, a third of the driving force behind existence would be gone. The fate of the cosmos after something so catastrophic is...quite bleak.

Dean nodded. "But, you said 'once before,' or something to that effect. It's happening again, isn't it?"

She sighed, tapping the cushion anxiously now. "I didn't want to believe it was so. I was not wholly honest when were below. The formation once only grew inches over the course of centuries. Now it is growing inches over the course of a few years. Its growth is accelerating, a little more growth and a little faster each year. That alone would not have been enough to make me worry, even with the growing chaos of the world with each passing year. But now you have come into the world, the first Child of the Sun in centuries. *That* above all else is what has confirmed in my mind that the Destroyer's madness has returned, and the Age of Darkness comes once more for us all."

Dean took an unconscious step back in surprise, "You think the return of the druids you talked about before is a sign?"

She nodded. "Yes. The last time the Destroyer attempted to swallow existence, there had been more shamans or druids than at any other point in time. Perhaps it is the other two beings who sought to create a balance of sort, or perhaps we are the defense of existence, of Gaia."

"I've heard mention of Gaia before, but I thought that was just the name for the planet...you werewolves used," Dean asked.

"Gaia is both the physical and the spiritual aspect of the planet. Some say that Gaia is just the ball of dirt and water with life upon it, while others say it is sentient and has a soul. Perhaps we are just pieces of her body, made to defend her when destruction threatens."

"Like an immune system," Dean added thoughtfully.

"Your awakening is no accident, to my mind. Any more than I believe that pieces of the crystal leaving here were an accident. Nox might have done so of his own volition, but he was a servant of the Destroyer, one way or another. I don't know if he was aware of the being he served, but he knew exactly what sort of power it was he sought."

Dean nodded. "Which brings me to the final reason I came here for answers. I need to find that final piece, and I have no idea where it is. Nox never mentioned what he had done with them and Damian didn't know. I need to find that crystal or it might fall into the hands of someone who knows what to do with it. I can't let that happen."

"Are you so quick to take on responsibility for solving the world's ills?" the Watcher asked.

Dean motioned to his group. "We know about the crystal and what it can do. Other than you guys, who have to stay here and guard what lays below, we're the only ones who know all that. If we don't do something, no one else can or will. It's not about being quick to take responsibility for anything. It's about the fact that someone has to do something or we're all screwed."

In response, she pulled a small chest up from the bench beside her and opened it. "Then I must give you these."

He stepped forward, eyeing the contents of the open box. It was simple, with a plush inner lining made from a material he couldn't immediately place. In it, were what looked like a chunk of clear class and a fragile glass vial of what looked like smoke.

"I'm honored by your trust, but...what are they?" he asked before reaching for them.

"The crystal you see is a piece of the one from below. All traces of corruption have been eradicated. And before you ask, that is no more a solution than destroying it. To purify even this small piece took many years and a great deal of strength. The crystal, even this small pebble's worth, is so attuned to the dark power that it would be an impossible task to cleanse it entirely. This small piece, however, will detect concentrations of the Destroyer's power. It will be enough that you will be able to sense the presence of a true servant of Him or of the crystal piece you seek. We do not have the means to find it wherever it may be, but this at least will provide a way to help."

Dean saw it had been pierced with a length of leather, making a necklace out of it, "How will I know? And how far will it detect?"

"Just as with the pieces you have seen before and the main formation below, it will begin to glow blue. The closer you are to the source of power, the brighter the glow. The stronger the source, the brighter the glow. It will lose the effects of the Destroyer's power with time, especially if you keep it close to your body. But beware, Dean. It will not stay pure if you should keep it exposed for too long. Use it as you will, but know that its usefulness could be lost quite easily."

It was peaceful and dull now, which meant that the crystal in the basement wasn't acting upon it. His eyes shifted over to the vial that lay comfortably next to the necklace. His initial thought of it being smoke was only partially correct now that he was closer to it. It now looked like a strange mixture of mercury and silver smoke rolling around one another behind the thin glass.

"And that?"

She reached out to touch the vial. "Shamans are capable, with the right training and the proper herbal mixture, to send their souls out from their bodies. It allows them to walk among the spirits in their own world, to speak and travel with them as they wish. The first of these walks was seen as a test of the shaman's skill and any that followed were seen as sacred rites, used to gain knowledge."

Dean eyed the shifting contents. "But I'm not..."

"No, you are not. As I said, a shaman could do so with the right training and herbs. Herbs that while not necessarily common, are usually simple to gather and mix. What you see before you is a mixture that would allow someone who is not a shaman to perform the same trick. The ingredients for such a mixture are tricky to find, and as such, rarely made. Or rather they were, but the knowledge of how to make such a concoction has been lost with the ages and this is the last vial we have."

Dean pulled back from touching the now even more fragile looking glass. "And why give this to me?"

"If there was ever anyone who could make the most use of this, it would be the first Child of the Sun in generations. To use it, you must pour it into water that was left to sit in the light of the full moon overnight. Then, all you have to do is breathe in the vapors from the mixture and you will walk as the shamans do. Again, I must caution you. It will work for one person, and only one time. The walk will take you where you need to go the most and you will learn much. Be sure that you only use it in a time of utter need."

She closed the lid on the box and placed it into his hands. Dean cradled it in his grip, trying to hold it without letting his nerves cause him to drop it. He hadn't expected gifts this powerful and rare, and he was touched by her sudden trust. They had come a staggeringly long way in the short time they had known one another.

"Thank you," he bowed, hoping the gesture translated properly. "You honor me with your trust. I hope I can prove worthy of it."

"That you intend to try is more than enough to bring me comfort," she smiled, reaching out to lay her fingers upon his hand.

"I will do more than that, I promise," he whispered fiercely to her.

She only nodded before drawing her hand away, "But, I am afraid that is all the help that we can offer. We do not know enough about the outside world to be able to do more than give you this bit of knowledge and these objects. I hope that it will be enough. I pray that it will."

They weren't exactly the solutions he had been looking for, but they were more than he had started this journey with. Both were powerful in their own right, but incredibly fragile as well. He thought that a fitting contrast since the world he was trying to save seemed much the same way. If the huge crystal below them was any indication, they were in for one hell of a fight if they didn't act quickly.

"I think it's time we head back, so that I can fulfill my promise," he told her.

"I imagine it is. You cannot save the world while locked away in our home, now can you? When you are ready, my people will escort you back to the point where you entered the jungle. From there, it is entirely in your hands."

There was a breath of relief from the table beside him. Dean glanced over to see that all of the group except Silun looked ready to go. The young man was staring down at the table, glancing nervously up at the Watcher. When his eyes shifted to behind Dean, where he knew the Learner was standing, a sad understanding filled Dean.

"I...there is one more thing you could do for me," Dean said, turning to face the Watcher once more.

Her eyes shifted to where his had been a moment before, returning with a smile. "Yes?"

"Would it be possible for you to allow my friend, Silun, to stay here for as long as he wishes, to learn from you? His training was interrupted when his master was killed and he was kidnapped. Now no other pack shaman will deal with us and he could use the training. That is, if he wants to."

Silun looked up, his face brightening as the Watcher looked at him. "Is that something you would want, young one?"

Silun looked at Dean nervously before speaking quickly. "If you would have me, I would be honored to learn from all of you."

"You have much to learn and it will not be easy," she continued, but Dean suspected that she had already made up her mind.

"If I'm...able to eventually leave to help my friends, I'll go through whatever you have in mind. Please. I'm almost useless like I am and I feel this would be a big help."

The Watcher turned to her granddaughter and spoke to her privately in their own language. Dean couldn't see the woman behind her, but he could see Silun staring intently at her. If Dean didn't know any better, he would think there was an eagerness in the young shaman's face he hadn't seen since he'd seen him look at Dante back in the Grove. That and he was pretty sure Silun was listening carefully, as if he had been learning their language a little and was trying to pick up what words he could.

"Very well, if you can keep up with the training, I see no reason to object. Perhaps it really is time some of our knowledge was let out into the world. We may just need it."

Dean smiled at Silun, who wore a torn expression of happiness and worry. If anything, Dean kicked himself for not realizing it was something Silun might have wanted to begin with. This was the perfect place for Silun to learn, even if it did seem to eat at him that he was going to be leaving in the first place.

"On that note, you had better ready yourselves. Your things will be returned and your escort waiting for you when you leave," the Watcher stood up to her full height, shoulders back. "I wish you Gaia's blessing in your endeavors, Dean. I hope what you have gained here is enough to give you the means to complete it."

CHAPTER 20

"I can't believe we're leaving him behind," Dante said, his complaining sounding a little depressed.

Dean watched Silun as he chatted with the Learner a few feet from them. "If this is something he wants, I can't really argue with it."

"Yeah, I know. I'm just going to miss the annoying little shit I guess," Dante said.

Dean smiled at him. "Why Dante, you almost sound as though you like him."

Dante rolled his eyes and moved away from them, to Dean's amusement. The guy might act like he was all hard and sharp edges, but that only made the moments when he was soft all the more obvious. He figured Dante was moving away to brace himself for the goodbye that was coming. Dean hoped it wasn't a forever goodbye, but it was a possibility they had to face.

"Dad is going to be so pissed," Mikael sighed.

Katarina crossed her arms across her chest. "Oh, he's always mad about something."

"Yeah, but he's going to blame Dean for this, again."

Katarina shrugged. "And then he and Dean are going to argue about it. They'll butt heads, realize they're both as stubborn as the other, and give up until the next round. Whatever good points Dean makes will be backed up by Mom and she'll make Dad realize that everything is fine."

"True, but you don't have to listen to them first," Mikael grumbled.

Dean turned on them with a glare. "Can you two not talk about me like I'm not literally standing a foot away from you? You two are worse than teenagers sometimes, you know that?"

"Uhh, what did I miss that Dean is chewing someone out again?" Silun asked from behind him.

Dean whirled around, feeling the heat coming to his face. "I wasn't chewing anyone out."

The Learner stood behind Silun, grinning at him. "Is he always this forceful?"

To Dean's complete dismay, everyone in the group, even Silun, echoed a simultaneous 'yes.' His outraged sputtering only earned him more laughter, to which he replied with the most dangerous glare he could muster. He knew they weren't complaining about him and they weren't really wrong, either. Dean knew full well that he could be aggressive, sometimes overly so, when he allowed himself to get fired up. It sure didn't mean he wanted to be called out on it, though.

Silun reached out and took hold of Dean's hand. "Thank you."

Dean looked up at him, puzzled. "For what?"

"For giving me this. I think it's exactly what I need. It's going to really help us."

Dean smiled weakly. "Don't thank me yet. Sounds like you're in for a rough road ahead of you here."

Silun shifted uncomfortably, glancing over Dean's shoulder. There was more he wanted to say it seemed, but the audience around them was making him uncomfortable. There was a general murmur of excuses coming from behind him, telling Dean the rest of his group was moving away. The Learner never said anything, backing up and returning up the stairs leading to the main entrance of the complex, where the group of her people who would be their escorts stood.

"I'm sorry," Silun whispered finally, sounding pained as he said it.

"Why are you sorry?" Dean asked, taking hold of Silun's hand and squeezing his fingers.

"Because I'm staying behind and leaving you guys. Leaving you. I told you I was going to help you with whatever you would be doing and here I am, choosing to stay here. I'm so sorry."

"Hey, you said it yourself when you spoke to the Watcher. What you learn here could really help us."

Silun shook his head. "And what if I'm here for years and you guys get everything all fixed? Then I would have just left you to do all the dirty work while I hid out here."

Dean's eyes fell on his pack beside him, where he had stowed the wooden box. "Something tells me that's not going to be very likely. If there's anything I've learned from the past year, it's that it never quite stops. There's always going to be something waiting for us around the corner that we have to deal with. Maybe you being here won't help us in the short-term, but think about what you'll be able to do once you're done here?"

"You think so?" Silun asked, a tremor in his voice.

Dean opened his mouth to speak, feeling the sting of tears in his eyes. "You know? You're probably going to be so much taller than me the next time I see you, more than you already are. You shit."

He had intended it to sound like a joke, something to break the depressing mood. It didn't work, his voice cracking at the end as he realized it was possible they would never see one another again. Silun's eyes filled up at the harsh sound, his grip tightening around Dean's.

"I'm really sorry," he repeated, voice wavering.

Dean shook his head, not wanting to cry but feeling like he would if they continued. He spared either one of them having to find something else to say and pulled Silun in for a hug. The young werewolf really was going to be big, probably as big as Mikael. He didn't seem to be much taller than Dean at that moment though, when he folded into his hug.

He pulled away reluctantly, keeping his hands on Silun's elbows. "And let me guess. You have a thing for a certain dark-eyed Learner?"

Dean wasn't surprised to see Silun's cheeks turn pink, "She has nothing to do with this."

"So, that's a yes?"

"Dean!"

He laughed, shaking Silun's arms. "I'm only teasing. I know you wouldn't want to stay here just because of a pretty girl. But don't think I didn't see you looking at her a certain way. The same way I've caught you looking at a certain werewolf: A grumpy, foul-mouthed tracker we both know."

Silun shook his head, fighting a smile. "Okay, maybe a little. It's not like I could hang onto liking Dante like that forever, could I? He's way older than me and he's not going to look twice at me in that way, not when...well, he's just not going to."

Dean stepped back. "Not when what?"

"It doesn't matter, just...take care of them for me, will you? I think Apollo will keep an eye on Dante, and you and Mikael will watch one another, but Kat? You should have seen her when we were surrounded Dean, she was...scary, and awesome. Someone has to have her back."

Dean glanced back at the woman, smiling. "We've all got her back, even you."

"Kinda hard to do that when I'm here."

"Well, you know what I mean. Even from a distance, you're still there for her, for all of us. We know what this means to you and what it could mean for the future. It hurts to leave you behind like this, but we all have to do what we have to do," Dean assured him, wishing he could take away the worry in Silun's eyes.

"I hope it's not for too long," Silun said softly, staring past Dean's shoulder.

Dean followed his gaze, seeing Dante and Apollo talking a fair distance away from any prying ears. "You going to be okay to say goodbye to him?"

Silun shrugged, looking just shy of miserable. "I said goodbye to you, didn't I? If I could get through that without blubbering like a baby, I should be able to manage with him, right? Plus, it's not like I'm saying goodbye forever. I mean it, Dean. I really do plan on coming back after I'm done here."

"I know," Dean said with a warm smile, even though he just wanted to curl up for a little while. He knew Silun meant what he said here and now, but that could change in the future. Spending even a year somewhere could plant roots for Silun, roots that would keep him here. Hell, the guy could fall in love with the Learner, settle down and have a few kids. Dean wanted Silun to be happy and fulfilled. He just wished it didn't come with the risk of losing his friend.

"I should probably talk to him," Silun said, shifting anxiously on his feet.

"Well, go on," Dean told him, turning so he could push Silun off toward Dante.

Silun glanced back at him, trying for another smile as he walked toward Dante. It wasn't a very effective attempt, but Dean returned the smile. Apollo noticed Silun's approach long before Dante did and stepped forward to speak quietly with Silun. They didn't talk long before Apollo walked away, leaving Silun and Dante to speak alone as he returned to Mikael and Katarina. Before Dean could do the same, he felt the sudden presence of someone standing behind him and turned around.

The Learner stood there, her eyes locked on him. "I've never seen a goodbye like this before."

Dean fought the urge to glance over his shoulder. "Even when you were out in the world like you said you've been?"

She shook her head, looking thoughtful. "The closest I have seen is people mourning for those they have lost to death. Our people do not depart from this place, save in death. I have never had to say goodbye to someone in life."

"Doesn't matter if you say goodbye to someone in life or in death, it still hurts. At least this way, he's doing something he wants to do," Dean told her, a lump rising in his throat once more.

"I hope we can make him happy here."

At that, he frowned up at her. "Speaking of which, as one of the only people he has left, I have to speak up. You guys trusted me with a lot so far, but I'm trusting you with someone important in my life. You understand that, right?"

Her thoughtful expression melted into a serious one. "I do."

"Good. Then you understand that if something happens to him, I'm going to be pissed. All of you had better watch over him and keep him safe. If something were to happen to him..."

He let the thought hang, but she nodded solemnly all the same. "I imagine we would be seeing you again. Though not with the hand of friendship extended."

"Is that serious or are you mocking me?" Dean asked.

The Learner shook her head. "No mockery. If there is one thing you fail in, it's that you sometimes do not think before you speak, yet you mean every word. It was not hard to see you are fiercely protective of what is yours and Silun is precious to you. We understand how important he is to you, and we regard you as a friend, even after this short time together. He is a friend as well."

"He's was busy while I was sleeping, wasn't he?" Dean asked.

She grinned at that. "Very. There is an attentive mind locked behind that sweet face of his. He does not yet know it, but there is steel in his spine, and he needs only to be shown it before he can use it."

"Sweet face, huh? You better not break his heart either," Dean warned.

She shook her head. "I intend to help teach him and to be his friend, Dean. No more."

Dean pointed over at Mikael, who noticed the gesture. "See that one? The one you've been checking out since we got here? I said the same thing when I met him: 'we're just going to be friends and I'll be perfectly happy just being friends'. Now look at us, so wrapped around one another it would take an act of God to pry us apart."

"Well, I think it's sweet. My people regard devotion and loyalty as the two highest virtues a person can have, and you two have that, in great abundance. If your fears were to come to life, I would hope I could attain even half the loyalty and devotion that you two possess for one another."

Dean felt the heat in his face rising, trying to keep his voice firm. "I don't fear that you two might end up becoming more than friends. If that happened, I would be happy for him, so long as he was happy. I just want him to grow, and be happy, doing what it is that makes him happy, and with the people who make him happy."

She reached out to rest her hand on his shoulder. "You are a good friend Dean, and as loyal a friend as you are a mate. All of you are, and he has been lucky to have you. Now it is our turn, let us try."

Dean snorted. "If I wasn't willing to let you try, I wouldn't have asked for him to be able to stay here in the first place."

He noticed she was staring beyond him and followed her gaze to see Mikael making his way over to them. "I'm glad you are trusting us that far. I think he will be a great student and a wonderful addition to our people for the time that he will be here. May your journey be safe and your mission fruitful, Dean."

She was gone again, leaving Dean and Mikael standing there as his mate stared down at him, trying to read the emotional weather on his face. Dean looked up at him, giving a half-smile that didn't quite reach his eyes. He was telling himself over and over again that this was the right decision, but it didn't change the fact it was breaking his heart a little to go through with it.

"You okay?" Mikael asked softly, sounding like he already knew the answer to the question.

"I feel like I'm letting him go to his first day of kindergarten, or that my best friend is moving across the country and leaving me alone," Dean said miserably.

"Does that make Silun your surrogate son and best friend?" Mikael asked.

Dean snorted, swatting Mikael's hip, "More like a little brother I think, and a best friend. He's one of the few people who's understood what it's like to try and figure out what it means to be different to everyone around you. His company has been...well, it's just been really nice having him around, and I wish we didn't have to leave him behind."

Mikael wrapped a comforting arm around his shoulder and squeezed. "You could ask him to come with us instead."

Dean shook his head. "You know I can't do that. This is something he feels he really needs to do and they can teach him more than we can right now. Honestly? It's the first decision he's made on his own since we found him, and that's a really good sign, isn't it?"

Mikael nodded. "It's a good thing."

"Just doesn't feel like a totally good thing."

Mikael chuckled, nuzzling his face into the top of Dean's head. "I believe they call that bittersweet, babe. But hey, it's not going to last forever right?"

Dean watched as Dante and Silun talked, standing away from one another. Neither man looked particularly happy. Even Dante was struggling to maintain the tough guy appearance he always kept up. Dean thought perhaps he wasn't the only one who felt like they were losing something like a little brother right now. Silun was openly miserable as he talked, his two hands clasped over one of Dante's. The sight made the lump in Dean's throat rise, even as he felt proud of Silun for the strength it must have taken to stay here.

"I hope so," he whispered.

CHAPTER 21

"So, we're out another shaman, then?" Samuel asked, voice tight with what sounded like barely restrained annoyance.

"He wasn't a fully trained shaman," Dean pointed out with what sounded like the same level of irritation.

"It amounts to the same thing."

Dean was tired; they were all tired. They had spent days wandering around the jungle following some vague directions, in the hopes they might find answers. They had found their answers eventually, but not without a lot of struggle. Dean had still been drained from his time fighting against the crystal's influence, only to have to face the difficult decision of leaving Silun behind.

Now, he was just as tired as the rest of the group, having taken the guided journey through the jungle, back to civilization. They barely slept on the flight back and had headed straight to the Grove to report everything to Samuel and Matalina. His exhaustion was making him less patient than usual, and he bristled at the blame he would swear he heard in Samuel's voice right now.

"It does not amount to the same thing, at all. This isn't the same as losing Talon, because last I checked, Silun is alive and happy where he's at. Because we failed to keep Talon safe, none of the other packs are willing to send one of their own to teach him, so I made the decision to let him be trained by people who would probably be able to teach him more. You weren't there, Samuel, and everyone seemed happy to leave all the decision making in my hands, so I made the damn decision," Dean told him, words hurried as his temper rose.

"There they go," he heard Katarina grumble behind him. Everyone from their party was sitting on cushions laid out for them in the Main House. Lucille sat with them, but the young woman was laid up in a chair that someone had dug up from somewhere. She was strong enough now to stay awake and talk, but not enough to hold herself up for too long.

"And did you ever consider that perhaps even a half-trained shaman would have benefitted us better now, rather than one fully trained a few years from now?" Samuel asked with narrowed eyes.

Dean snorted. "He wasn't even a member of this pack, Samuel, so you had no command over him."

"Considering the nature of him coming into our hands, and the fact that we have yet to hear from his pack, he might as well have been."

Dean sighed. "So what, you're so eager for a shaman now that you wanted to snatch up and claim the first one that came your way?"

Samuel's nostrils flared. "I was not claiming what wasn't mine, Dean. I am *not* Damian, and I am not anything like him. Watch what you say."

He threw up his hands in frustration. "Samuel, if I

thought you were anything like him, do you really think I would still be sitting here trying to be a part of this pack? I didn't mean that you were anything like him, only that it's that kind of behavior that gets people into trouble. You can't sit there and try to claim that I handed over a member of this pack when we both know Silun never was. He was only under our protection until we found his pack again. At the very least, you could only accuse me of handing over someone who we were supposed to be keeping safe."

As was her custom, Matalina leaned forward to interrupt. "And you truly believe that he will be properly trained by these people you found?"

They had found him, but he didn't think that was an important distinction right now. "I do, completely. They have knowledge about things we never dreamed of, and in some ways, I wish I could have stayed there a bit longer to learn more. If he stays there for even a year, he would come back with more knowledge than we could dream of. Silun is smart as hell and he's eager to learn. Whenever he comes back, he'll be one of the best trained shamans that anyone in our corner of the world has ever seen."

Matalina glanced at Samuel who shrugged slightly. "Do you think he will come back?"

"I don't know," Dean answered honestly.

"That's not exactly inspiring confidence in this decision Dean," Samuel huffed.

"I wasn't trying to make you feel better about it, but I am being honest. We all went, knowing there was a chance some or all of us might not come out of there. Well, it went better than expected, since we're all alive. If Silun being there means a possible better outcome in the future, then I think it's the best thing we can hope for."

There was another moment of silent communication

between the two Alphas. Dean didn't even try to figure out what was being shared between them. Much like he and Mikael, whatever was being silently communicated was nothing he was going to be able to interpret. It was still a little strange to see, and he wondered if that odd mixture of brow movements and quirking lips, was how he and Mikael looked when they did that.

"If this provides Silun with the education and training that we have been unable to provide him, then we can only hope that it is the best decision," Samuel said with a tone of finality.

"Told you," Katarina whispered to Mikael.

"Something to add, Katarina?" Samuel asked sharply, glaring at his daughter in the way Dean wished he could.

Mikael's snorted and Katarina stiffened. "Not at all, Father. Just tired and thinking out loud."

Samuel didn't look convinced but shifted his attention back to Dean. "Do you think what you learned will be of any use?"

Dean ran his fingers over the small chest that sat before him. "It was the best they could provide and I really hope their best is enough. I know what they told me wasn't necessarily the definitive answer we were all hoping for. But we're all dealing with a bunch of old legends and blurred myths, so it shouldn't surprise us that there wasn't anything concrete they could tell us."

"Is that you telling me it wasn't a useful trip?" Samuel asked.

"I think it was extremely educational and we learned what was at stake. Trust me when I say we don't want that crystal piece to remain lost. I saw what could happen if it was left to grow unchecked and now I have a better way to find it than I did before. And if that doesn't work, I have a backup option that can hopefully guide me to an answer."

Matalina was staring at the chest in thought. "What peculiar objects of power! I never dreamed such things were still in existence. Rumors and stories spoke of old objects that possessed fantastic abilities, but it's something else to know they exist, still. Are you certain they will work?"

Dean shrugged. "Unless the Watcher was a great actress or just ignorant, I believe she gave me two things that will work for me. I don't know how well they will work, but there's only one way to find out. We won't know until they're used, though."

"So, just as before, we sent you all on a vaguely guided mission, and you came out with a success that could possibly not be a success?" Samuel asked.

Dean couldn't help his grin at that. "Now you know how blind I've felt while trying to figure out how to get my powers to work."

"And what do we do about the crystal piece that we have?" Lucille asked quietly from her place beside them.

Dean turned to her. "Use a silver weapon to destroy it. There's nothing more we can learn about it and it's better that it's gone before someone learns we have it and tries to find some way to get a hold of it."

"And what of the container it is bound in? I believe no one has yet been able to open it," Lucille continued.

He winced. "It's probably a good thing no one was able to. It's better that it's just destroyed and be done with it. Nothing good could come out of being around that thing for too long, trust me. Even a small piece could be dangerous around people."

"I think Lucille should be the one to destroy it," Mikael said.

"Why?" Samuel asked.

"Because it sounds like she already had to deal with its effects once before. It's probably what put her in that coma, and she's the one who found it in the first place. Makes sense that she's the one to destroy it too," Mikael answered.

There was a certain poetic justice in that and Dean could appreciate it, so he threw his support behind it. The rest of the group extended their own support for it, with varying degrees of certainty. Dante and Katarina sounded like they were agreeing simply to move things along, probably dreaming of finding somewhere to curl up and fall asleep for days. This journey had been no less exhausting than the last one, and they were all ready to crawl out of here and find a hole to hide in for a little while.

Samuel seemed to sense that they had reached their limit, straightening to his full sitting height. "With that settled, I'll end this meeting. This may not have gone the way any of us had hoped for, but it's good that you are all safe and alive. Leave and go get some rest, I will need you all to be in your best shape soon."

Happy for the reprieve, Dean knew he still had to ask. "And what of the search for the other piece of the crystal?"

Samuel shifted. "Much like the crystal we have now, what we will do about that piece will have to wait."

Dean sat completely upright,."With the one we have now? You need to destroy that one, Samuel!"

The Alpha held up a hand. "Patience, Dean. I have been listening to your warnings and taking them very seriously. However, I had a thought that we need to know just how well this gift of yours from this Watcher will work. If we can figure a way to extract the crystal we have now from the tube, we could then use it briefly to measure the extent of this object's abilities."

Dean's protest died on his lips as he thought about that for a moment. He could see the logic behind wanting to test the sensing crystal's abilities. It was, after all, an unknown object, one that the Watcher either hadn't been able to, or simply hadn't measured its capabilities exactly. With the active piece of the dark crystal they had now, they could conceivably use it to see if the crystal worked at all, and just how well. It would mean not having to wander around everywhere hoping it might work at some time.

The practical part of his mind accepted it as justified, but there was still the wary part of him that screamed to rid themselves of both the tube and the dark crystal. He had seen, twice now, just what an unchecked crystal could do. It would only be out of its casing for a brief time, long enough for them to experiment with the sensing crystal the Watcher had given him. Still, that felt like too long for him.

Finally, he spoke up. "I'm not totally comfortable with the idea of leaving the piece we have around. But I can't really argue with the logic of what you say either."

Samuel looked amused. "As Alpha, I have total say of what happens to it, so I'm glad that you aren't going to fight me on this, for once."

Dean rolled his eyes, no longer caring if it was disrespectful. "I have perfectly good reasons for being cautious, Samuel."

"And so you do. However, I also have my reasons for continuing to keep hold of the piece as well."

"Will you at least make sure that it's kept hidden and safe?" Dean asked.

Samuel scoffed. "As if I haven't already. As I said before, I have been listening to your warnings about the crystal and I've taken them very seriously. The only people in this pack who know of its existence and possible importance, are the ones in this room. The tube has been kept locked away, without any of us acknowledging it."

That, at least, was somewhat comforting, since he knew the best way to hide something was to pretend it didn't exist at all. It didn't take away his fear of what it would mean if the crystal wasn't destroyed soon, but at least it wasn't a tantalizing prize for all the world to know about. They didn't need another Nox, or Damian for that matter, aspiring to get their hands on the crystal, by any means necessary. The pack had dealt with enough consequences of power-hungry aspirations to last them a lifetime, or two.

"Satisfied?" Samuel asked, doing a good job of hiding any caustic tone.

"No, but I don't really have too strong a reason to object now either," Dean said bluntly.

"Good enough," Samuel said with some amusement, dismissing them finally.

When they emerged into the sunlight of the Grove, Dean took a deep, soothing breath. Without thinking about it, he extended his senses out into the woods around them. The comfort of the familiar surroundings flooded him as the deep calm and patience of the forest filled him. The trees were still doing their whispering with one another, and he could sense the little plants growing diligently on the forest floor.

After spending so long dealing with the overwhelming strength of the jungle, it was wonderful to feel the age of the forest again. It was in no hurry to go anywhere, as it had been here for eons. It demanded nothing, and the life within it was absent of the driving hunger the jungle possessed. Things here were in balance as they should be, and it was exactly the sort of thing he knew they were working to protect.

"Zoning out again?" Dante asked as he brushed past Dean to catch up to Apollo.

Dean didn't bother to respond, since Dante hadn't bothered to slow down at all. Rolling his eyes, he watched as Dante slipped up close to the quiet scout, slipping an arm around his back and walking away with him. Dean watched as Apollo unconsciously leaned into the touch and Dante's fingers curled into his side.

Something bubbled up in Dean's mind and was interrupted by a bump to his shoulder. He looked over to see Katarina beside him, with Lucille at her side. The small woman was holding herself up by gripping onto Katarina. Both of them looked exhausted, but he could also see in them the stubborn refusal to admit it. Once again, Dean found himself wondering if that sheer stubbornness was a werewolf trait or just one that ran in the family.

"I didn't get to say it before, Lucille, but I'm glad to see you on your feet," he told her.

She smiled at him, looking grateful. "It has not been a particularly fun road, but recovery never is. I find that it's also exceptionally boring, very repetitive. Hopefully on your next grand adventure, I will be well enough to join you."

Dean laughed. "Well, hopefully that won't be for a while yet. It sounds like your dad hasn't quite made up his mind about whether he wants to send us out to look for that other piece just yet."

"You don't agree?" Lucille asked neutrally.

Katarina scoffed. "Of course he doesn't agree. Dean and Dad almost never agree on anything, haven't you noticed?"

"It would be hard to miss," Lucille said, eyeing her older sister with a wry expression.

"You guys make it sound so...bad," Dean huffed.

"No, not bad. Father has always been a strong personality, so he has had to be to do what he does, and do it well. I do not necessarily think it is a bad thing that he must now contend with another strong personality," Lucille said.

"Better answer than Kat gave. I think she just likes watching us butt heads sometimes," Dean accused.

"Hey, it's funny!"

Lucille ignored her. "Other than Mother, there hasn't been anyone who could bring themselves to stand against Father. You have never been intentionally disrespectful, nor have you disobeyed him, so I see no problem with it. If anything, the two of you compliment one another even in your adversity. Both of you are the whetstone for the other's blade."

"That's...one way of putting it," Dean said slowly, put off-balance by the odd thought.

"It doesn't hurt that you have done much for our older brother as well. I don't believe I have seen him quite as happy as he is now. I'm sad that I missed so much, but I am happy to see that the results have been wonderful."

Now he just felt awkward but was spared from having to reply to her earnest praise by the sudden presence of a body behind him. Even without the sudden waft of a familiar scent filling his nostrils, he knew it was Mikael. His mate pulled Dean back into him by his waist and held him tight in a hug. He felt Mikael sag against him slightly, the only show of his own exhaustion that he was willing to give and only to Dean, and it made Dean smile.

"Here or yours?" Mikael asked, trying for a sultry tone and missing by a mile.

"Ours," Dean corrected, turning so he could see Mikael's face. "Think we have the strength to drive back?"

"If it means being able to sleep for as long as we want without being dragged out of bed, I have the strength for any amount of driving," Mikael told him.

CHAPTER 22

Dean flopped lazily on the couch, staring up at the ceiling and knowing that he needed to get himself motivated. He and Mikael hadn't bothered to do much of anything since they returned to the farm. As a matter of fact, they had spent most of their time in bed. It hadn't been all about sleeping, and Dean was pleasantly sore as a reminder. There had been the trips to the kitchen for food of course, but they hadn't done a single, productive thing since returning.

His coming into the living room rather than returning to the bedroom had been Dean's attempt at motivating himself to do something. It hadn't worked too well once he sat on the couch and laid himself out. He knew full well there was still plenty of work to do on the farm, but it didn't seem all that important at the moment. The farm grew well enough without his help, since apparently being a druid meant that everything grew spectacularly. It was a bad idea to rely on that in the long-term, but he couldn't be bothered to worry over it right now.

The other downside to being on the couch rather than

either working or crawling back into bed next to a sleeping Mikael was that he was left alone with his thoughts. Their last adventure had left him with more questions than he'd had before. Despite how angry Samuel had seemed about it, he didn't regret leaving Silun behind, and it was the one thing he was sure of. He didn't know if waiting to find the other crystal and leaving the one they had intact was such a good idea. Then again, he didn't have a good idea of where to even begin searching, and that was something else praying on his mind.

He couldn't call their mission a failure. They had gained more knowledge about what had happened in the past and had walked away with possible tools to help them in the future. He didn't know if that was going to be enough, though. Mikael had been a nice distraction, drawing him into the present rather than worrying about the future. It meant that as he lay alone, everything he had been putting off simply rushed in to antagonize him.

A soft knock at the door brought him out of his thoughts. He heaved himself up off the couch and padded toward the front door. Dean was glad that Jax was such a heavy sleeper when he curled up in bed with them, other-wise the dog's barking would have woken Mikael up. Dean might have to deal with his own worries, but he didn't see the point in waking Mikael up when he was sleeping so peacefully.

When Dean swung the door open, to his surprise, he saw Apollo standing on his porch. No one else was with him and Apollo didn't seem anxious or worried. If anything, Dean thought he looked more well-rested and content than Dean had ever seen him, especially after Artemis had died.

"Apollo?" Dean asked, opening the door wider and gesturing for the scout to come in.

"Did I wake you?" Apollo asked as he stepped in.

"No, was just being lazy on the couch, thinking about what we still have to do. So, you kind of saved me from myself. Everything alright?"

Apollo wandered into the living room. "Hm? Oh, yes, everything is fine. Everyone has been taking the time to relax and get their strength back and I thought I should check on you two. Where's Mikael?"

Dean pointed up as he sat. "Sleeping. It's kind of all we've been doing."

Apollo raised a brow slightly, but said nothing. Dean waved at him dismissively, knowing the gesture for what it was. If it had been Dante, it would have been a crude and overt joke about how they had been doing a lot more than sleeping. Apollo didn't even need to say it, as Dean could see the joke shimmering behind his almost impish expression.

"Don't start," Dean warned him, earning him an innocent expression.

"You said you were thinking about everything. Do you need to talk about it?" Apollo asked.

Dean shook his head. "No, not yet. I need to think about it alone for a bit before I talk to anyone about it. Thank you, though."

Apollo nodded in understanding and lapsed into his familiar silence. After the man had stayed with them, Dean had become adept at reading him. There was an uneasiness in Apollo that hadn't been there before. Dean had the sense that Apollo wanted to say something, but had to work himself up to speaking the words aloud.

Dean decided to help him along a little. "Is there something you want to talk about?"

Apollo shifted in his seat slightly. "Me? What makes you ask?"

Dean snorted at the evasion. "Okay, well how about I help you? Because I think I know what's on your mind."

"You do?"

"Probably the same thing that had you on my front porch looking more peaceful and happy than I think I've ever seen you. Let me guess, you and Dante?"

Apollo looked startled, the open emotion looking strange on his face. "You know?"

"I wondered for awhile now, if something was going on. But it hit me that something really was going on after we met with Samuel and Matalina back at the Grove."

Apollo frowned. "What could have given it away?"

Dean shrugged. "Nothing big that I could point at and say 'there, that is what made me know.' It was a bunch of little things that have built up over time. You guys have been so close for so long, so that's what started it. You act differently around him than you do us, and I think Silun knows too, by the way. He's part of the reason I suspected."

Apollo smiled a little at that. "He's very perceptive, isn't he?"

"Knows more than he lets on, kind of like you. Since I'm pretty sure you noticed how Silun was about Dante, too."

The werewolf nodded. "I think Silun was aware that I knew, and I think it made him feel uncomfortable around me. It wasn't necessary, but I understood."

Dean chuckled. "I bet you did, since you both had a thing for the same guy."

Apollo looked away. "It wasn't anything I planned to happen."

Dean dropped his amusement when he saw how uncomfortable Apollo was. "Hey. I'm not saying you went into this with a plan, alright? But that's how things work out sometimes, especially between friends. Same thing happened with Mikael and I. Why do you sound like you're trying to place blame on yourself over this?"

Apollo raised one shoulder and let it drop. "I just worry that I might be ruining a friendship."

Dean shook his head. "Or, you might be bringing something wonderful into your life. Look, Dante might be a bit of an asshole. Okay, a lot of an asshole, but if being with him makes you happy, why worry about it?"

Apollo tried not to smile. "He can be a bit...difficult at times."

Dean waved a hand at him. "And then some, but that's not important. I've seen how he is with you and that whole 'My name is Dante and I'm a total hard ass' thing of his goes right out the window when he's dealing with you. I don't feel the slightest twinge of worry about the two of you being an item. I've seen how he is. If he softens up that much with you, even when other people are around, I can only imagine what he's like when you two are alone."

For the first time since the start of the conversation, Apollo brightened up. "He's completely different to the way you know him, I promise."

"Good, then what's the problem? Just because you two were friends before this? I knew someone who swore up and down that was the only way to have a good relationship. You two have been close for years, so that's a really solid foundation."

Apollo looked down at his clasped hands. "And if it goes wrong? What happens to our friendship, then? I worry what it might result in if things don't go well."

Dean snorted. "Look me in the face and tell me you believe you two would really stop being friends if this didn't work out? Do you really think he would turn his back on you?"

Apollo looked up, still uncertain. "You speak as if you know him well enough to ask that."

Dean shook his head. "I don't, but you do."

Apollo nodded, letting that sink in and going silent once more. Dean could see he was still undecided as to whether it was a good idea or not. He could understand that. It had to be a scary situation, becoming romantically involved with your best friend. Dean didn't want to push him to continue if Apollo thought it would truly be a bad idea for he and Dante to carry on. Yet, he could see the happiness that Apollo was feeling because of it, even if it was mingled with anxiety.

"Okay, look, here's a few simple questions you need to answer. Does he make you happy? Does he treat you well? Can you see a future with him like you guys are now?" Dean asked.

Apollo took a moment to look up and meet Dean's eyes. "Yes, to all of them."

Dean threw his hands out before him. "Then why worry? Just feel happy instead."

"I am happy," Apollo said, sounding like he meant it.

That admission took away most of the worry lines forming on Apollo's face. Dean could see the happiness Apollo was feeling more clearly now, mingling with a hope that probably scared him. Dean knew all too well what it was like to be so hopeful for something you felt could be wonderful, while fearing what would happen if it crashed and burned. It wasn't easy to put yourself on the line like that, and Apollo had been through a lot lately. Dean thought maybe more love in his life would do wonders for the scout, especially after having lost so much.

"So," Dean began, grinning a little evilly. "How's the sex?"

At that, Apollo straightened and for a moment, Dean thought he had upset his friend. It wasn't until he saw the beginnings of color in Apollo's cheeks that he realized he had embarrassed him instead. He couldn't help the chuckle that bubbled up out of him as he realized Apollo was apparently a little shy when it came to sex. Well, his own sex life anyway, since the man had no such reaction when it came to living with Mikael and him, and dealing with their sex life.

"I'm guessing that it's really good," Dean pushed.

Apollo's eyes narrowed slightly. "I don't think that's really an appropriate conversation, do you?"

Dean laughed again. "Oh come on, Apollo! You got to know everything about Mikael and my personal life while you were here, so let me have a little peek at yours now!"

"You say that as if I intentionally sought out the knowledge that you two are like teenagers, teenage rabbits at that."

Dean couldn't argue with what he felt was an accurate, if crude description. He also knew that Apollo was just deflecting so he was no longer the focus of the topic of conversation. Dean grinned wickedly, leaning forward and refusing to let Apollo escape so easily.

"Is he hung?" He asked, going for the jugular.

"Dean!" Apollo protested, sounding so mortified that Dean felt a little bad for embarrassing him so easily.

"Fine, fine. I'm sorry," Dean sighed, flopping back into the couch once more.

"I really do not want to talk about him like that," Apollo said, sounding a little huffy.

"Okay, I won't ask about his size or skill, or anything like that. I do want to know if it's good for you, though."

"Why?"

"Because whether people want to admit it or not, that's a big part of a happy relationship between two sexual people. Chemistry is a big deal," Dean answered honestly.

Apollo sighed, bending slightly before Dean's logic. "Alright. Yes, the sex is...good."

"Good?"

"It's wonderful," Apollo amended, looking pained to have to even speak the words aloud.

Dean grinned wide at the admission. "So, you got with your best friend? Even had sex and...wait a minute, is *that* what the tribespeople found so funny when they found you? Were you guys...?"

Apollo's cheeks colored even darker. "I don't want to talk about that. Bad enough that we were surprised."

Dean couldn't help his chuckle, covering his mouth so he didn't embarrass Apollo too much more. "I'm sorry, I don't mean to laugh. It's just...that's awful. They saw you guys?"

Apollo's jaw tightened, and Dean realized he was pushing him too far. Apollo had come here to talk about something that had been preying on his mind, and Dean was taking too much amusement out of it. He straightened his features immediately and reached forward to take Apollo's hand in his own.

"I'm sorry, I really am. I'm not trying to make fun of you, really I'm not. I'm genuinely happy for you and I'm glad he makes you happy. I've been a little worried about you for so long, you know that?"

"I've been better," Apollo said quietly.

"I know. You really have. You're tough, and you've been doing really well, but it doesn't mean that you've been as happy as you deserve to be. If you being with Dante helps you be that way, then I'm all for it, okay?"

Apollo smiled gratefully at him. "Thank you, Dean. I appreciate that. I didn't realize when you came into Mikael's life that you would be such a big part of mine as well. I consider you my friend and I'm proud to call you that."

Warmth flooded Dean. "I'm glad we feel the same way, Apollo. You all have become both family and friends to me, and it's great to see you getting what you deserve, finally."

A thought seemed to occur to Apollo and he looked up at the ceiling. There was a nervousness in his eyes that Dean noticed immediately. He squeezed Apollo's fingers reassuringly, shaking his head when Apollo looked at him.

"Don't worry. I won't say anything to anyone about what we just talked about," he told him.

Apollo sagged in relief. "Thank you. I don't want everyone to know until...Dante and I are a little more sure of everything. I don't think he's talked to anyone about it, but I think I just had to tell someone."

"For someone who doesn't say a whole lot most of the time, that's a pretty big deal. That you came to me over it is a big deal. thank you."

"It feels good that someone else besides us knows about it. After everything that has happened, and what lays before us, it's been...wonderful to have something like this in my life. Even if it does worry me at times," Apollo admitted.

For a moment, Dean's mind pinged back to the thoughts he had been having before Apollo showed up. There was still a lot to worry about, especially if the lost crystal turned out to be in the wrong hands. They still didn't have a solid plan for how to deal with that, and Dean knew that he wouldn't know any peace until it was settled. That he now had to think about the Watcher's words about the Darkness returning wasn't helping, either.

He brought himself back to the present, grinning wickedly at Apollo. "True, but at least now you have really hot sex to distract yourself from all that other stuff."

"Dean!"

Dean laughed at that, forgetting his worries for the moment as he shared in his friend's happiness. The world might be headed towards some dark catastrophe in the near future, but he had so much to think about right now. Everything else would have to wait, because he had his mate and his new family to surround himself with. That would be enough for the present. The future could wait.

90594545R00134

Made in the USA
Columbia, SC
05 March 2018